M... Marauders

Geraldine Hennigar

Illustrated by
Ivan Murphy

Nimbus Publishing Limited
P.O. Box 9301, Station A
Halifax, N.S.
B3K 5N5

Design Editor: Kathy Kaulbach
Project Editor: Alexa Thompson

Nimbus Publishing Limited gratefully acknowledges the support of the Council of Maritime Premiers and the Department of Communications.

Except for the mention of Al Capone, Elliot Ness, General James Wolfe, Joseph Howe, and Billy Bishop, all characters in this story are fictitious.

Hennigar, Geraldine.

Midnight marauders

(New Waves)

ISBN 0-921054-70-X

I. Murphy, Ivan. II. Title. III. Series.

PS8565.E56M52 1991 jC813'.54 C90-097706-X
PZ7.H46Mi 1991

Printed and bound in Canada

To Gerald W. Sinnis,
who encouraged us to be inquisitive,
and Mrs. E. (Betty) Sinnis,
who said our goals are attainable.

Contents

1
To the Rescue

"The kittens go," said Mrs. Veinotte. She wet her thumb and forefinger at the water pump and tried to flatten an unruly roostertail at the back of Dan's blond head.

"Ah, Mom...."

"No, Daniel, two cats are plenty." Mrs. Veinotte wiped her hands on her apron. Then, cupping her son's chin in her palm, she stared into his grey-blue eyes. "I have enough to think about. Your new brother or sister will be here before we know it...."

Dan knew that once his mother's mind was made up not even a northeast gale could sway her. But this baby thing was getting under his skin. For the past eleven years, life at the Veinotte home had been perfectly satisfactory—why add a pampered package that would cry all night?

"Go on dear, or you will be late," encouraged Mrs. Veinotte, her voice a little softer. "And remember to meet me at the church gate after school. I'll need your help to carry home the church linen for washing."

"Don't worry, I'll be there." Reluctantly Dan left. It occurred to him that years from now the memory he would have of his mother would be of her standing in the doorway, shooing him off to school.

Dan dragged his feet along the rocky dirt path. His breakfast of oatmeal and milk lay in his stomach like a lump of clay. He would have sulked all the way to school but a familiar sound cheered him up.

"Trinkets, trash, and treasures!"

It was the rags-and-bones man. Dan had a feeling the peddler would likely stop at his house for a bowl of the morning porridge. Dan turned around, jumped off the path and crawled like a monkey over the damp, yellow grass back toward his home. The knees of his breeches were soaked through, and he scowled at the dull, spring sun that tried to warm Nova Scotia's South Shore.

Dan hid behind the outhouse. From there he could watch Seaport's most persistent peddler pushing his oversized wheelbarrow full of pots and pans and a jumble of useless articles along the village road. It was Robert MacIsaac though no one called him by his real name. Shortly after the war he had started drinking and soon became known simply as Corker, after the corks in his favorite rum bottles. Already on this mild April morning, the man was hot and tired. Removing a black derby hat, Corker wiped his brow with his ragged coat sleeve. A large Newfoundland dog, its tail wagging and a wet tongue hanging from the side of its mouth, plunked its haunches down by its master.

Men down on their luck—and there were a lot drifing across Canada in 1931—soon knew the doors in any town that were good for a hand-out. They even left signs to let others like themselves know where to stop. Corker eyed the two broken bullrushes crossed to make an X.

"Stay here, girl, and guard me valuables." Hobbling off the road he headed up the path to the small bungalow with the large porch.

The peddler tapped out a lively tune on the back door. Dan popped his head around the corner of the outhouse just as his mother appeared in the doorway.

"Mornin', Missus," said Corker cheerfully. "Any odd jobs for a weary vagabond such as meself? Or perhaps the lady would fancy something from me select merchandise." With an air of grandeur he waved his hand toward the cart beside the road.

"Well, now." Marie Veinotte glanced over her shoulder at the box by the woodstove. "There are the new kittens. I already have two good barn cats. I'll give you twenty cents to get rid of them for me."

"Say no more. 'Tis kinder to be rid of the wee creatures than have them starve," said Corker. Noticing her anxious face, he removed his hat and held it close to his heart.

In a moment Mrs. Veinotte returned, with a wriggling burlap sack in one hand and a few coins in the other.

Dan blinked away tears. He did not want to cry but the kittens were so helpless. He waited until Corker had gathered his wares and moved away from the house. Then, scrambling over the grassy hill, Dan jumped the ditch in time to meet Corker and walk with him along the road.

"Mornin', lad," called Corker. He set down the red-chipped handles and rested against his cart. "Can I interest you in anything this fine spring day?"

"I'd like to buy...." Dan hesitated. He let the dog lick the salty sweat from his hands.

"A hoe, perhaps?" Corker reached past the sack and pulled out a badly chipped garden hoe.

"No."

"A tractor seat? Good for a bike."

"Some other time."

"I know," said Corker, wetting his finger tips on his lower lip, "a pair of boots, and I did say *pair.* Usually I only carry one at a time." Proudly he held up two unmatched boots, laced and held together with twine. Bits of straw poked through the soles.

"No, no," shouted Dan. Then, trying to get control of himself, and the situation, he added more calmly, "Say, what do you have in that sack?"

"Kittens, that's it!" sang Corker. He put his arm around Dan and drew his face close. Dan could smell the stale tobacco and rum on his breath. "I was paid handsomely to drown 'em. Seems almost criminal."

"Yes, it does," Dan agreed eagerly. "I could take them off your hands."

"Well, lad, I made the lady a promise and I'm not one to go back on me word. Ah, unless the price is right." He looked craftily at Dan.

Dan reached into his pocket and withdrew a dime, a nickel, and three pennies—enough to keep him in hard candy for a month.

"I'll give you eighteen cents for the kittens," he announced.

"Oh, my." Corker scratched the grey stubble

on his chin. "I suppose, mind now, your mother won't like it, but I'm not one to snitch. So let's trade lad, before I change me mind."

"You knew!" blurted Dan.

"Yup, saw ya behind the outhouse." Corker chuckled. He pocketed the money and handed Dan the sack of kittens. With a tip of his hat the peddler pushed his cart down the road toward the village. Corker was feeling hungry. Today he would have a real meal, one served hot on a plate and set before him on a table with a fancy checkered cloth. It would taste like a slice of heaven after all those bowls of soup from the handout kitchens. The dog followed, her tail wagging in rhythm to her master's happy whistle.

Dan was left alone to mull over his dilemma. Why had he been so fired up to save the kittens? His mom would not take them back, he had no food for them, and....

"What's that ya got?"

Dan swung around. He had been so absorbed in his thoughts that he hadn't heard Becky Wentzell approaching. She stood with one hand on her hip, the other pointing to the sack.

"Just kittens," Dan replied casually, his mind busily plotting a scheme.

"Why are they in that sack?"

"I've been asked to drown them. Seems almost criminal."

"Sure does," agreed Becky.

"I'll have to do the job, but if the price is right you can have them."

"Look who's the criminal!" shouted Becky. "You know very well I don't have any money. I was going to offer to take the kittens home—but go ahead, do your nasty job." Head held high she marched away, her white pinafore swishing wildly over the tops of her laced boots.

Dan was sorry he had mentioned money. Becky's mother had been widowed twice, and the villagers referred to her fondly as the Widow Wentzell. He knew they had no money to spare since the Widow's second husband, Becky's father, had been swept overboard last summer during a storm.

His own father had once told him that the Widow's first husband, Charlie Mader, had been one of more than three thousand Canadians who had lost their lives at Vimy Ridge. That battle had been in 1917, a year before the end of World War I—long before Dan and Becky were born. A few years later, the Widow had married Willie Wentzell. The couple had three children—Becky, who was a year younger than Dan, and two smaller boys. The Widow had a lot of mouths to feed.

"Wait, Becky, I'm sorry," called Dan, running after her. "It would be swell if you could take the kittens. I wasn't ... I wasn't going to drown them, honest. My mom says they have to go. Please, Becky, please take them! Food won't be a problem. I'll fish off Whynott's wharf every day."

Becky stopped marching. She peered into the sack. "All right. Your mom isn't going to like it if she finds out, but I won't tell." Grabbing the sack she headed back toward her house, her red pigtails bobbing in time with her marching feet. Without looking back she shouted, "Tell Miss Spindler I'll be a few minutes late for class."

Dan watched her cross the field. "The morning certainly is off to a good start," he thought. "I've disobeyed my mom, given away my candy money, and said 'please' to a girl."

2
Day Off

If Dan's morning had been sliding downhill, the afternoon took a welcome swing upward.

Bang! Bang!

"Class, ignore that noise. As I was saying…"

Bang! Smash!

"Halifax, the capital of Nova Scotia is…."

Crash! Tink … Tink!

Muffled giggles filtered across the room. Miss Spindler scowled at her students. In the little school house all the students from grades six to ten sat in one room.

"Who's making all that noise?" asked Becky Wentzell.

"That," replied Miss Spindler proudly, "is the workmen in the cellar installing the new coal furnace." She realized that for the first time during the history lesson she had everyone's attention. "We will be the first two-room school in the county to have a furnace."

Dan eyed the pot-bellied wood stove that sat in the far corner of the classroom. Although the teacher talked on excitedly about modern conveniences, he felt sad. Each morning during the cold months the students brought kindling to school. Most dreaded trudging knee-deep through the snow on freezing winter mornings and coming into a cold school house. Not Dan—he liked warming it up. He especially liked being fire monitor. Fire monitors were allowed out of their seats at any time to stoke the fire. Now, because of Miss Spindler's interference, the school had bought a coal furnace. At that moment Dan hated his teacher.

"Joseph Howe is a name to remember," said Miss Spindler, returning to her lesson. "And this weekend you should read...."

Tap ... Tap ... Boom!

Suddenly a choking cloud of sooty smoke billowed from the vents. Instantly a mass of screaming, laughing children stormed out of the grey school house.

Classes were over for the day and Dan Veinotte was having second thoughts about the new furnace. Maybe it wasn't so bad after all. Children fanned out in all directions. Dan took his usual route. Circling the school, he plodded through the Wentzells' hay field and scooted across Eisnor Road. The other boys had arrived at the vacant dirt lot, ready to play baseball.

Bruce Bealer yelled at Dan as usual, "What took ya so long? Get out to centre field. OK, Squirrel, let 'em rip."

Squirrel stood on the upturned sod of grass that was used as the pitcher's mound and chewed nervously on his lower lip. His eyes widened, then narrowed. A long leg rose, a gangly arm swung back. Then, like a released coil his whole body except for one foot whipped forward. The ball sailed toward the batter. Bruce swung—and missed.

In the outfield Dan snickered. He knew Bruce could not hear him. No one laughed at Bruce Bealer and went unscathed. He had once belted Craig Jollymore for taking his hat by mistake.

"Too high," bellowed Bruce, "I ain't no giraffe."

Squirrel wound up again, more nervous than before. The second pitch dipped and rolled over the cardboard batter's diamond and into a wet gully.

"Sorry," mumbled Squirrel, "I'll get it right next time. An off day." The truth was that he had the best pitching arm in Seaport. He got plenty of practice, because Bruce made him throw for both sides to keep the game going. Still, sometimes Squirrel wished he could have a turn at bat. Just once he'd like to hit a home run zinger.

"Ya, and you'll fetch the ball too," ordered Bruce. Squirrel snapped out of his reverie.

"I'll get it," said a voice from the edge of the hay field. It was Becky. She always watched the games. For the life of him Dan could not understand why. Every day it was the same.

Becky would ask to play, then Bruce would snap his suspenders against his chest and snarl at her.

"No girls allowed. Your mommy is calling you. Beat it!" Bruce raised his bat threateningly.

Becky's lower lip began to tremble. Slowly her muddy fingers released the ball. It landed directly in front of Bruce's big, brown boot.

Dan pretended not to notice. He emptied loose gravel from his shoe. She might be a decent player, he thought, but Bruce was boss. No one liked it that way, but only a fool would suggest a girl be allowed to play—and Dan was no fool. The shortest kids were always sent to the outfield to flounder after the ball. It wasn't much fun being in the outfield, chasing after the ball and being called names. Dan wished he was taller. His mother promised he would have a growth spurt and he hoped it would get here soon.

"Go home. Go home." Bruce taunted Becky.

Soon everyone, including Dan, took up the chant. His insides felt hollow, like the sickening feeling just before a big math test. Then he remembered his mother was waiting at the cemetery. He was glad to have an excuse to leave the game.

"Gotta go," he shouted, as he turned to jog down Eisnor Road.

"Come on, stay awhile," whined Squirrel. "I want a turn at bat."

"Na, gotta go. See ya tomorrow." Bruce swore and Dan picked up his pace.

He headed for the Anglican church. It stood on a rocky cliff like a white angel defying the dark waters that crashed like a thousand demons along the jagged coastline.

Marie Veinotte was waiting by the wrought-iron gate. One brown curl whipped across her forehead, the rest of her hair was hidden under a plaid scarf. A strong wind pressed the worn green sweater and long wool skirt against her slender body.

Dan could not believe his mom was expecting a baby in five months. It hardly looked as if a baby was growing inside her belly. Dan remembered when Mrs. Countway was expecting her twins. She had spent the afternoon in the Veinotte's kitchen, exchanging local gossip and dunking crisp molasses cookies into black tea. When the visit was over it took both Dan and his mother to pull Mrs. Countway and her belly up and out of the chair.

"Hi, Mom," called Dan. Secretly he hoped she would have sense enough to stay at home when she began to show more. It was selfish, but he could not help feeling the way he did. He didn't want the other kids to stare at his mother.

"Hello, Daniel. I'll take the starched linens inside and gather up the soiled ones." Faithfully, each Friday, Marie made sure the altar was properly dressed for Sunday service. Soon she had finished her chores and was closing the big oak doors. She found her son in the cemetery standing over Martha-Rae MacIsaac's stone. Close by was a tiny mound. Here lay Corker's wife and child. Marie put her arm around Dan.

"Mom?"

"Yes, dear?"

"They died on the same day—November 11, 1918."

Marie sighed. "Yes, it was the very day the terms of surrender were signed in Europe. I was eighteen at the time. Martha died giving birth to her baby. Poor Corker didn't know. He returned home to find his wife and child buried." Marie reached out to trace the moss covered letters. "If only Corker could find comfort in the Lord and not in the devil's brew."

For the rest of the afternoon Dan's thoughts were troubled. He tried to understand why Corker drank too much and washed too little. It was sad to think no one loved or cared for him. But it was difficult to imagine the death of Corker's wife and baby. Dan was glad nothing so tragic had happened to his family.

3
Treasures

Later that evening Dan waited impatiently by the kitchen window. A journal, given to him by his mother, sat untouched on the wooden table. To cheer up her son, Marie turned on the radio. However, tonight not even Dan's favorite program, the hockey game with Foster Hewitt, interested him. There had been word from one of the local fishermen that his father would likely be home sometime this evening. Five days was the longest Nick Veinotte had ever been away on any chase, and Dan missed him terribly.

"Come away from the window," scolded Marie. *"A watched kettle never boils."*

A dog barked in the distance. Could it be?

At last Dan recognized the familiar footsteps on the porch. The door flew open and Nick Veinotte's broad shoulders filled the entrance. Dan bolted across the room, scattering papers in every direction. Even at eleven he enjoyed a bear hug and a whisker rub. In one swift movement Nick reached out and drew his wife into the circle.

Dan looked into his father's eyes. "Dad, did you catch any smugglers? Did you tie up the rumrunners? I bet they cried when you dumped their hooch overboard?"

Nick's hearty laughter filled the kitchen. Marie slipped from his arms to serve up a late dinner which she had kept warm on the back of the wood stove.

"No, not this time," answered Nick. He hung the red uniform jacket on the door hook. "Came close though. We knew the mother boat, carrying her cargo of rum, was sitting just outside the twelve mile limit. Some nights there are so many boats the boys and I call it Rum Row." Nick bent into the sink to wash.

"What's the twelve mile limit?" asked Dan.

"That's the limit of Canada's control of the seas off the coast," Nick explained. "We can't arrest boats outside the limit."

Dan stood so close that water from the pump splashed on his face too. He loved his father's stories. When Dan was younger the tall tales were about pistol-carrying pirates wearing eye patches. Since Prohibition, when the sale of liquor had become illegal, the characters had changed to shotgun-carrying sailors in slickers. Even the treasure had changed. Instead of a bounty of gold bullion, the catch was smuggled rum.

Nick winked. To please Dan, he made the job of Preventive Service Officer sound exciting. But the long, cold, damp nights enlivened by occasional fast chases did not suit Nick's slow, easy-going nature. Still it brought in an honest pay.

"Go on, Dad. How come you couldn't catch them?"

Nick sat down at the table. "Night after night we waited and watched as smaller vessels crawled out to the mother boat like ants to honey. Finally we thought we had one with liquor on board. We were sure we could nab her. We chased that schooner clean down to Shelburne where she dropped anchor."

Dan sat on the edge of his chair.

Nick continued, "We gave the boat a thorough search but there was no sign of any liquor on board. Guess she lived up to her name."

"What was her name?" asked Dan.

"The Lady Luck," replied Nick grimly.

Disappointment washed over Dan's face.

Nick ran his fingers through his thick hair. "I think they dump the liquor at sea and then haul it up again later, when the coast is clear. But how they locate the cases of liquor, I haven't a clue."

"Dad, let me go on a chase!" begged Dan.

"Certainly not," said Marie, as she set a steaming dish of sauerkraut and sausages before her husband.

"Maybe a day cruise sometime," whispered Nick. Closing his eyes he inhaled the pungent aroma of pickled cabbage. "Ah, my favorite."

"Dig in while it is still hot," ordered Marie. "And Daniel, give your father a bit of peace while he eats."

Dan and his mother had eaten earlier. To keep still Dan sat on his hands and chewed the inside of his cheek. He had something else he needed to tell his dad, something important.

After Nick had swallowed the last drop of tea, he pushed his chair from the table and reached for his pipe.

Dan thought it safe to speak. The bottled up words popped out of his mouth in one great gush. "Dad, I heard the music again last night. It's coming from the Widow Wentzell's, I'm almost sure."

Nick and Marie exchanged a concerned look. For the past two months Dan had told them he was sometimes awakened at night by a mysterious moaning melody. It drifted into his room on the evening breeze and invaded his dreams. Because Nick and Marie shared a bedroom on the oceanside of the house, they heard only the sound of waves breaking on the beach.

The mysterious music began shortly after Marie had announced her pregnancy. She thought that Dan, who had become accustomed to being an only child, might have invented the music to get attention. Still, Daniel had not lied to her before. Maybe the Widow Wentzell was up to something.

"I hope the Widow is not selling bootleg liquor," said Marie. "Times are hard but an honest living is the right living."

Nick shook his head. He pulled a pouch of tobacco from his pocket and set it on the table. "If contraband liquor is finding its way to the Widow's, my boys and I will eventually find out where it's coming from. It isn't the seller, but the supplier, we're out to catch."

"Dad?"

"Yes, Son."

"Why is it called bootlegging?"

Nick scraped the bowl of his pipe with a dead match stick. "As the name suggests, Daniel, fishing slickers and rubber boots are plenty big for stashing bottles. Oh, almost forgot, Son—I brought you home a little something." Reaching into his shirt pocket, he drew out a coin.

"Wow," sang Dan. "Pirate's gold?"

"It is whatever you want it to be," said Nick.

Although the date was worn, the coin resembled the Spanish Bolivar Dan had seen in his book of rare coins.

Marie smiled at her son's delight. "Go on outside and play for half an hour. Don't be late."

Dan jumped into his rubber boots. Grabbing his knitted sweater he ran out through the door to the back porch. He raced down the winding dirt road that followed the shoreline of the small fishing village. The promise of an early spring scented the mild evening air.

Perhaps it was because Corker's family was still on his mind that Dan, as if pulled by a magnet, was drawn back to the Anglican cemetery. Sitting in the grass he let his thoughts drift—everything seemed so peaceful. Gradually dusk inched its way across the night sky. The music floated so softly that Dan hummed a few bars before realizing the notes were real. On a clear night sound can travel a great distance over the cold Atlantic. He hugged himself and recalled stories of graveyard skeletons shaking their bones. "No," he thought, "the music seems to be coming from across the field."

He could see the dark outline of the Widow Wentzell's house in the distance. A movement caught Dan's eye. Someone was leaving. A dwarf-like figure crossed the field—coming his way. Quickly Dan jumped behind Mrs. MacIsaac's stone. Cautiously he peeked around the winged cherub and immediately recognized the figure.

Corker's tattered derby covered one eye. A large potato sack, slung over his back, tinkled with each hobbling step. The second intruder of the night entered the cemetery. As the old man headed for his wife's grave, Dan ducked behind the headstone.

Corker plunked himself down on the plot, then reached into his overcoat for a plug of tobacco. Soon tobacco juice dribbled down his chin.

Here

Adjusting his belt, he cursed his bad leg that had been injured during the Great War.

"Ah, Martha me dear, how are ya this evenin'?" Corker took a drink from a small flask, wiped his face on his sleeve, and spat on the ground. "I still miss ya even after all these years."

If a night owl had been watching, it would have seen an odd sight—an old man slumped against the gravestone, and only inches away, a young boy huddled behind it in fright.

Corker continued the one-sided conversation. "Tonight I made me usual drop. Now darlin,' I know ya don't approve o' me methods, but I tried to make an honest livin.' No one would hire a retired soldier with a bum leg. Travellin' them box cars all across Canada ain't no way to live. And it was too far from you. Aye, it was. And them bread lines, no dignity, no sir."

The speech was a long one for Corker. He stopped to refresh himself from the flask. "Now I ain't stealin,' and I ain't cheatin' anyone, 'cept maybe the Government. Anyway, it could have been you left strugglin' and not Charlie's widow. As soon as I keep me promise to him I'll stop." Corker leaned a little to one side. "Well, yes, I do fancy teasin' the Feds."

Dan knew "the Feds" was a reference to his father and the other Preventive Service Officers. It could mean only one thing—Corker and the Widow Wentzell were involved in illegal rum smuggling. But what was the debt Corker had mentioned? Dan grew more curious and less nervous. Again he peeked around the stone.

Corker closed his eyes, jerked back his head, and downed the last drop of rum. When his eyes opened they gradually focused on something shiny lying on the ground. He groped with one hand and picked it up.

"Martha, what do we have here—payment for me humble services? Looks like an old coin."

Dan fumbled in his pocket for the coin his father had given him.

Corker held out the coin as if to show it to his deceased wife. "Life, Martha, is like treasure. Then fate comes along and gambles with it. Heads I win, tails I lose." He flipped the coin into the air and missed it—his reflexes had been slowed by the liquor.

"Lost again. Guess coins and rare treasures, like you dear, were never meant for me to keep." Sighing, Corker gathered his bundle together. Then, to Dan's horror, Corker took a few steps and disappeared over the edge of the cliff.

4
A Mystery

Dan crawled toward the cliff. The thunderous crashing of the waves pounded in his ears. He was terrified of finding Corker's broken body on the rocks below. Slowly Dan peered over the edge. But Corker was nowhere to be seen.

Although it was time to be heading home, Dan had to find out what had happened to the old man. As he looked more closely at the cliff face, he could see knotted tree roots and what might be—must be—a path.

Carefully, he turned and lowered himself over the edge. The rock felt ice-cold and Dan had the urge to let go, to fall slowly backward as if in a dream. "Hang on," he told himself. He felt with his boots for a firm foothold and found himself on the path. It led downward and around an outcropping of dark granite, then disappeared from sight. Ahead of Dan was a crevice in the cliff, large enough to climb through. He peered into the hole and found that what lay below was like nothing he had ever seen or imagined. The crevice was a natural skylight for a sea-carved room below. For hundreds of years the pounding waves had gouged out a secret cavern. The last of the day's sunlight reflected through the water at the cave's narrow mouth. Dancing shadows cast eerie images on the bluish-green walls. Dan's heart fluttered like a whirl-a-gig. Dripping water had made the tree roots slick as grease and he hesitated to go farther.

Below him, Dan could see Corker awkwardly lower himself down the cave wall. The old man swung around and climbed into a waiting boat. She was a black Cape Islander, trimmed in green and badly in need of a paint job.

Suddenly the excited bark of a dog echoed throughout the cave.

"What's the matter, girl?" Corker asked the

big Newfoundland dog. "Not worried about the Feds tonight? They can't put a crimp in our style." He reached out to untie the line. As the engine cut in Corker pushed off and headed the boat for the mouth of the cave.

High above, Dan tried to piece together the events of the last hour. Somehow the Widow Wentzell and Corker were tangled up in a rum running ring. But where was the evidence? Dan had three things to go on—music played only at night, an overheard conversation, and an empty cave. "It's not enough," he thought. Luckily tomorrow was Saturday. He would have to keep his eyes and ears opened for more clues.

Dan made his way back up the path, and over the cliff. A blast of sea air sent chills over his body. It was mild however, compared to the frozen look he got from his mother when he returned home late. Dan knew without a doubt that he would be punished in the morning.

Exhausted from the fresh air and physical exertion Dan threw off his clothes, climbed into his flannel nightshirt, and fell onto his bed. Something sharp stuck into his back. It was his journal. Quickly he scrawled in the entry for the day: *April 14, '31, Dad is home. Gave me a new coin. Lost it in the graveyard. Corker and the Widow share a Seaport secret.*

Dan fell into a deep sleep the moment his head hit the pillow. He dreamed that large musical notes slipped in through the bedroom window, wrapping themselves around him like a cozy cocoon. Effortlessly they lifted his body into the air. Floating like a cradled baby, Dan drifted out of the window and upward toward the crescent moon.

Next morning a bucket of hot soapy water, a long handled shovel, and a scoop of lime waited downstairs for Dan. Cleaning the outhouse was the ultimate punishment.

It was nearly noon before Dan finished his dismal duty. He left his sloshy galoshes on the back porch. In the kitchen Marie and Nick chatted about local news.

"Relight the stove please, honey," said Marie.

"I'll serve up your pork scraps and cod cheeks—a good lunch for my night marauder."

"I hope she doesn't think up things to keep me busy all day," thought Dan. He had some serious investigating to do. He reached for the morning paper to crumple up and stuff in the stove. The headline caught his eye: April 15, 1931 *CAPONE'S TRIAL SET.*

"What have you got there?" asked Nick.

"Says Al Capone, from Chicago, is going on trial for not paying his taxes," answered Dan.

"That gangster launders his dirty money right here in the Maritimes," said Marie, as she scraped the iron frying pan. "Is tax evasion all he'll get nailed for? Now that's a real crime!"

Dan was puzzled. "Dad, how do you wash money?"

Laughing, Nick reached for both his son and the paper. "That means he likely buys illegal liquor with money he made from gambling. That way the police can't trace the money back to him. There are some men 'round here willing to sell him illegal rum." Nick glanced over the news article. "Wait now, it seems a Federal Agent, Elliot Ness, has arrested the man who kept Capone's record books—perfect evidence."

"Dad?"

"Yes, Son?"

"Why would anyone here want to work for a man like that?"

Nick took a deep breath, "There are people who have no jobs, little money, and a family to feed. Running a little rum across a border or over territorial waters can put money into men's pockets that might otherwise be empty. But for others it's plain greed."

"If the lesson is over," interrupted Marie, "there is one more errand, Daniel, then the day is yours."

"Oh, Mom!"

"Take this bundle of clothes you have outgrown over to the Widow Wentzell's. She may be a strange one but the Lord tells us to love our neighbor, strange or not."

Dan was glad to go. He would pretend to be Elliot Ness and piece the clues together. Maybe at the Widow's place he could find out something about Corker's strange activities of the previous night. The two, it seemed, were in cahoots. Two plates of pork scraps and cod cheeks disappeared in record time.

5
Clues

The Widow's two-storey, grey-shingled house, perched on a hill, was badly in need of repair. Shutters hung haphazardly on their hinges. Forgotten window boxes held dry, broken flowers. Dan made his way through the hay field that grew up to the doorstep. He could hear the squeals of play-fighting from the younger children.

Dan gave the weathered door a timid tap. First a girl's giggle could be heard, then Becky's mop of red hair appeared. Her blue eyes sparkled. Dan shifted uneasily. How was it she could make him lose all his confidence with just one look?

"Ma, it's Dan Veinotte," called Becky, without taking her eyes off him. Still giggling she reached out and, grabbing his coat sleeve, drew him into the house.

"Bring the boy inside," answered a woman's husky voice.

"Yes, Ma." Another giggle.

Dan stepped into a long, dark hallway. An oak hat rack, hung with scarves and mittens, stood guarding the entrance. Peeling wallpaper curled from several cracks in the wall. On the floor were braided rag rugs.

Suddenly two bodies, arms flailing, legs kicking, tumbled down the rickety stairs from the landing.

"No fair!"

"I'll get you."

"Catch me first."

Jess, who was six, seemed to have the advantage over his older brother. First one, then the other, pushed roughly past the visitor.

Dan wished the Widow would hurry up. Between Becky's goggly-eyes and her brothers' noisy fighting, he was slowly suffocating.

Then out from the kitchen marched the familiar, short, square body. The Widow

Wentzell didn't look at all like his own mother. Her red hair was cropped like a man's. Black piercing eyes sat close together above a short, turned up nose. She stood with one hand stuffed into the pocket of a pair of men's trousers, the other hand outstretched. The only person who had shaken Dan's hand before was the Reverend Samuel Rhuland.

"From Mom," said Dan, handing over the parcel. His whole body shook from the hearty handshake.

"Ah, yes," she replied.

She seemed to Dan to be expecting the clothes. The Widow had the reputation of knowing people's business before they did! "She has to know about the secret smuggling," he thought.

"A big thanks to both your folks," said the Widow. "Can you stay for tea?" Without waiting for a reply the Widow turned and headed for the kitchen.

At that moment the young wrestlers raced by again, and Becky smiled.

"No, can't, thanks. Gotta go," said Dan. The

place was just too busy, unlike his own quiet home where his mom kept things in their place and where you could hear yourself think. He fumbled for the door latch. If this was the way a house was with younger kids, then why did his parents want another baby? He jumped through the doorway, broke into a run and did not slow down until he had reached Whynott's wharf.

For now there was a whole afternoon to do whatever he liked—and it felt like a fishing day. It was a good thing he had bought a supply of twine from Bob's Dry Goods Store earlier in the week. Corker's con job had depleted his funds. With crushed snails for bait Dan could try his hand at jigging for flatfish. After all, he did promise Becky fresh fish for the kittens. With a whistle on his lips he skipped to the end of the wharf.

Dan seated himself on an up-turned fishcrate and threw his line into the clear water of Mahone Bay. There was nothing like fishing to soothe troubled thoughts.

In the protected inlet several boats lay

moored to their buoys. They turned one way until the tie-line grew taut, then slowly swung in the opposite direction with the moving tide.

After a while two men appeared from the cabin of one of the boats—a sleek schooner. One stuffed a rolled-up piece of paper into his yellow slicker while the other readied the dory tied to the stern. As they rowed ashore Dan caught snatches of their conversation.

"Hugh, are you sure ya got tonight's spot marked?"

"Yes, Tom, I've got the chart right here in my shirt."

"The chart ain't no good if we need to sail with the lights out!"

"Don't worry, I've been studying the shoreline and the islands. I'll have my bearings before...."

The dory approached the wharf where Dan sat idly fishing and the conversation was suddenly cut short.

"Here, boy," ordered the one named Tom. He tossed Dan the line. "Give us a hand."

"Yes, sir." Dan caught the line and tied a

bowline around the nearest post. It was low tide and the men had to climb up the ladder on the side of the wharf. Without a word of thanks to Dan they headed off to the village. Dan thought about the times his own parents had abruptly stopped talking when he entered a room. Were these men discussing something he was not supposed to hear?

Dan returned to his fishing. He looked out to sea. Boats and masts were reflected in the blue water. A few feet away greedy seagulls squawked as they fought over chunks of rotting mackerel.

He thought about last winter when he had gone smelt fishing with his father. They had sat out on the bay under a tarp and fished through a hole cut in the ice. The smelt ran for three weeks in December. One day, much to his mom's horror, they hauled in fifty-two of the bony little fish. Nothing could beat a feed of smelt rolled in flour, fried in butter, and smothered in onions, golden crisp on the outside, soft and white on the inside. The smelt were running again but Dan knew better than to eat the spring run. They had as many worms as they had bones. Hopefully the flatfish were healthy. He stretched out his legs and let several lazy hours pass.

All at once the boat the two men had left swung gently and Dan noticed the name of the schooner. *"Lady Luck,"* he said aloud. Wasn't that the same boat his father had chased to Shelburne and had suspected of carrying illegal liquor? What was it the two men had said—something about a marked spot? Some detective he was. Elliot Ness would have seen the clues right away. Maybe it wasn't too late. Dan had overheard some important information. Perhaps his dad could use it to get the evidence needed to nab the smugglers. He must hurry.

Dan balled the wet twine and stuffed it under the fish crate. Tomorrow was Sunday and he might get another chance to fish. His feet took flight and his head was filled with ideas.

The sight, in the distance, of a Model A Ford car parked in front of his house brought Dan back down to earth. Only a couple of people in the village owned a motor car. This one belonged to Doc Jollymore. Something terrible must have happened.

6
Trouble

Dan raced for home. A sickening feeling gnawed at his empty stomach. He stopped short of the porch, reluctant to go into the house. Had his father been hurt while chasing ruthless rum runners? Dan knew boats loaded with illegal liquor also carried guns. The smugglers tried plenty of tricks. They sometimes put oily rags over the exhaust pipes of their engine, then, behind a barrier of black smoke they would out-manoeuvre the Federal cutter. But if they couldn't elude the law, the smugglers would use their guns.

Dan lingered by the Doc's Model A Ford. He kicked the right front balloon tire. One foot on the ground, the other raised, he hop-stepped along the running board.

What if it wasn't Nick the Doc had come to see? Dan recalled the morning his mother had been frying ham for breakfast. Suddenly she bolted for the back door. Dan had never heard his mother sound like that before. Nick had chuckled, "Morning sickness, all part of pregnancy. With you, son, it was the smell of liver and onions." Dan never could swallow the brown, rubbery stuff without gagging. Maybe as an unborn child he had already known how awful liver tasted.

The car window was rolled down. Dan reached inside to feel the rumble seat's ribbed material. Next he rubbed the round, bald head of the three-speed gear stick. It would be great to fly along full speed—at fifty miles an hour.

At the sound of the screen door creaking, Dan snatched back his hand as if the gear stick was suddenly red hot. Quickly he jumped off the running board and ran up the porch steps.

He reached the back porch in time to catch Doc Jollymore's words of advice. "Rest is what she needs. I'll be by later." Tipping his hat he left.

"Mom?"

"Glad you are back, Son," said Nick. "Come and sit down. I've made some tea." Nick cleared his throat in an effort to steady his quivering voice. "Your mom has had a miscarriage." A little tea spilled into the saucer.

"A what?" asked Dan.

"Sometimes a woman loses her baby," answered Nick.

Dan could understand losing a shoe, or misplacing his homework. Once he felt really bad when he lost his best jack-knife—but to lose a baby!

"How?"

"Something went wrong, Daniel. The baby arrived too early to live. Let's go up and see your mother for just a minute."

Mechanically, Dan's legs carried him up the stairs. Had he wished so hard for the baby to go away that it had actually happened? Was the concern in his father's voice and the sadness in his eyes his fault?

Father and son tip-toed into the room. It was quiet, too quiet. Dan looked at his sleeping mother. Although she looked pale, she was beautiful with her long hair spread out over the pillow.

In contrast, his father looked haggard. Tufts of salt-and-pepper colored hair stood out here and there. Lined, rough hands gently stroked his wife's arm. Dan walked out of the room backward, wanting to pretend this hadn't happened.

He drifted into his bedroom, a place where he could be alone. The walls closed in around him like a prison cell. Perhaps that's where he belonged. Then he tried to imagine what it would be like to be dead. Perhaps he'd be better off. At least he wouldn't have to face his parents. But dead is not being here anymore. After a long time, he reached for his journal.

Saturday, April 15, '31. Mom's baby is dead. The kid was born before he was big enough to live. Why did this have to happen? I wish I hadn't thought the things I did.

A noise from the kitchen below interrupted

his writing. Dan went into the hall and poked his head into his parents' room.

"Perhaps it's the doctor returning," said Nick, without looking up. "Go down, Son, and see."

But it was not the doctor. Dan was surprised to find the Widow Wentzell rummaging through the cupboards. She had piled an assortment of potatoes, carrots, parsnips, and a turnip on the table.

"What are you doing?" asked Dan.

"I'll boil up a mess of stew. It ought to keep you and your dad going for the next few days. Now don't give me that lost pup look. Your mom will soon be up, good as new."

"Why did this happen?" Dan's words were a whisper.

"Lord only knows," replied the Widow. The fingers of one hand flipped a potato while a knife in the other hand licked off the dirty brown peel quick as lightning.

"Just doesn't seem right. How can God let people get sick and die?"

The Widow understood Dan's frustration.

She set down the paring knife. "Dan, that was not what I meant." How could she make an eleven-year old boy understand his mother's miscarriage had nothing to do with him? "God, gives comfort. He does not take it away." She looked into the troubled face. "Dan, reach into the sack and get me two more potatoes."

Dan crossed the kitchen. He looked over last year's crop and chose two potatoes that were still firm and had not grown roots. The Widow waited and watched as he set them down on the table.

"Why did you choose these two?"

"They were the best I could find," replied Dan.

"Exactly," said the Widow. "That is the way I figured it. When both my husbands went the way of the Lord, I reckoned He gained two of the best."

"Seems a little unfair to me," said Dan.

Plunk—a carrot cut and quartered, hit the pot. The Widow leaned forward, eyes wide, lips pursed. "Sometimes there are consolations. Do you believe in ghosts?"

"I ... I don't know," stammered Dan.

"Well I do!" The note in her voice confirmed her belief. "Sometimes Charlie—that was my first husband—speaks to me."

Dan sat down. "How do you know it is him?"

The Widow glanced around to make sure they were alone and continued in a whisper. "One night, while I was playing *our* song on the piano, I heard him singing along. In a hollow voice—that likely comes with being dead—he called out my name. Of course I thought it was my imagination ... but he and I were the only ones to know what that particular song meant to us ... and now he comes back to visit regularly. He provides for me—so I can manage in these hard times."

"The mystery music," thought Dan. He had not imagined it! But was there really a ghost or was the Widow covering for someone?

At the sound of Nick's footsteps the Widow straightened up.

"Not a word," she whispered.

"Ah, Mrs. Wentzell," said Nick. "Good of

you to drop by. I'll take a cup of tea up to Marie."

"Dad, can I talk to Mom?" Dan wanted to promise her he would never be so selfish again.

"Sorry, Son, she's still groggy from the doctor's medicine. Give her time to rest." Nick took the tea the Widow had poured and slowly climbed the stairs.

There had to be something Dan could do. He stared at the Widow's broad back as she leaned into the sink, sure that somehow Corker and the Widow were connected with the *Lady Luck*. Something was definitely going on tonight. Someone had to get some answers and, since his dad was busy, it would have to be him. While the Widow's back was still turned he slipped out of the door and headed for the cemetery.

7
Stowaway

Dan eased himself over the precarious ledge. On reaching the entrance to the cave he crept in backward like a sandcrab entering its home. His eyes needed time to adjust to the grey-black world inside. A cold, musty smell filled his nostrils and soaked into his clothes. A monotonous plink-plunk of dripping water echoed throughout the belly of the cave. Below, sat Corker's boat, the sea water slapping her bottom noisily like a painter's brush.

It took forever to inch down the slick granite wall. Now Dan could see the name of the boat—*Martha-Rae*. Where had he heard that name before? Then he recalled the tombstone and the sad story of the woman and the child.

Martha-Rae was the name of Corker's wife. It occurred to Dan that today he might have lost his own mother. The thought wrenched his guts worse than a punch from Bruce Bealer.

He remembered the dog. "Here, girl. Nice dog." When neither the dog nor its master replied, Dan climbed up and over the side of the boat onto a bench which ran the length of the stern. He moved slowly around the large engine box that took up most of the deck and pushed open the door to a tiny cabin in the bow. Inside was a tangled heap of rope, fishing lines, and a smelly fishnet. Propped against the ribs of the hull were two bags of coarse salt. "Corker must fillet and pack fish on board," thought Dan. A pile of canvas made a comfortable seat; one of the salt bags served as a pillow. He would wait here for Corker to return. Snug and warm inside the cabin Dan felt the day's problems slip away and, rocked by the gentle waves, he soon fell asleep.

The sudden sound of a man's heavy boot on deck caught Dan by surprise. On impulse he flipped the musty smelling canvas over himself and lay still, hardly daring to breathe.

First he heard the dragging boot of the lame leg, then the sound of "Hawk-tu-splat" as black tobacco juice hit a tin can, and finally the grinding of the engine coming to life.

"Why is this door open?" growled Corker.

Slam! Click!

Corker headed the Caper out to sea. Inside the tiny cabin, Dan lay like a trapped rat. Perhaps it was all a bad dream—soon he would wake up to his mother's call for breakfast. He removed the canvas but still couldn't see anything in the dark cabin. When his body began to lurch with the rolling movement of the waves Dan knew he was in real trouble.

As the *Martha-Rae* left the cave to ride the choppy Atlantic waters the engine throttled into a full roar. The noise hurt Dan's ears, but the ride did not last long. Dan guessed they had stopped at Whynott's wharf since it was the one closest to the Anglican Church. He pressed his ear against the door.

"Come, girl," called Corker. The excited bark

of a dog answered as it bounded aboard.

Men's boots thudded across the wharf. Dan heard voices.

"Did ya mark the spot?"

"Aye."

"I don't want your fish on Monday. Can ya remember?"

"Aye."

"Nine sharp!"

Dan couldn't hear the rest of the conversation. The dog scraped her claws frantically at the cabin door. She broke into an earsplitting howl.

"Settle down, girl, or I'll leave ya behind," threatened Corker. "You'll be giving away our location."

With a crank of the engine he headed the boat once more out to sea.

Inside the cabin the stowaway wrestled with his fears. What would happen to him if he was discovered? Well, he had no intention of revealing himself. Dan figured the men had made a rendezvous for rum smuggling. That was what the conversation he had overheard was really all about, he decided. Detective Veinotte was back on the case.

Dan judged the time to be about six o'clock. That meant he faced a good three hours of noisy, rocking darkness. If nothing else, it gave him plenty of time to think. He thought about the Widow and her comforting words about his mother. If he could blame God for what had happened he'd be off the hook. But that thought didn't make him feel any better. He had to think about something else. What about the midnight music? Was it really used to lure a ghost? The Widow had mentioned a secret that helped her through these times when jobs and money were scarce. Then Dan remembered he had seen Corker slip through Wentzells' hay field just last night. It seemed more had happened to boggle his brain in the past two days than in all the dreary winter months put together.

The cabin grew hot and stuffy. Once or twice Dan drifted off into a state of semi-sleep. Only gnawing hunger kept him from nodding off completely.

After what seemed like a thousand hours the engine died. The boat bobbed in the water then bumped against something. There were more voices.

"My salt is wet."

"I don't want your fish on Monday."

"Is that you, Corker?"

"Aye, ya lazy landlubber. Let me aboard!"

"By all means," answered the voice. "We'll seal the deal with a tot of rum. Leave the loading to my boys."

Dan heard the clump of boots moving across the deck. He pressed his back into the rib of the hull and drew the canvas up over his head. The door swung open. The light of a lamp made a quick sweep of the cabin.

"OK, Hugh, start passing down the load."

That voice! That name! Where had Dan heard it before? One man began to whistle a tune. A clinking crate was crammed into the cabin. It landed on Dan's foot.

"Ow!"

Instantly a pair of strong hands reached in and grabbed Dan. At that moment Dan

recognized his captors. As he dangled in the tight grip of the angry smuggler, all thought of heroic detective work vanished.

8
More Trouble

Dan stared into the rugged face of the rum smuggler. Accusing eyes peered out from under bushy black eyebrows. A snarling lip curled to reveal tobacco-stained teeth.

"Ha, Tom, I've found me a spying rat," snarled Hugh. "He's just a waif but he'd make good shark bait."

"Let me go," cried Dan.

"Do as he says," ordered Corker. He hobbled over the deck of the mother boat and climbed down onto the *Martha-Rae*. "You boys let me deal with me lazy deck hand."

Had Dan heard him correctly? Did Corker call him his deck hand?

With a sweep of his arm Corker dismissed

the two rogues. Roughly he pushed Dan toward the stern of the boat. He lifted the seat and shoved Dan's face into the storage space.

"Rules are if ya come aboard, ya do your share of the work. Start stashin'."

"Yes, sir!"

The twinkle in the old man's eye, and his confident handling of Tom and Hugh, helped Dan to relax a little. He knew he had been plucked from the grasp of pirates and this was no time to ask questions. The Newfoundland dog rubbed a friendly greeting against his leg. Eager to oblige Corker, Dan set to work. Rum bottles, each wrapped in a potato sack, were handed to him to be fitted under the seat. Meanwhile, Tom and Hugh finished loading crates into the cabin. The switch of cargo from one vessel to another took only a few minutes. It was time to shove off—for where, Dan could only guess.

"Now kindly get off me boat," said Corker. The workers grunted their indifference to the order and returned to the mother boat, a fine schooner that Dan judged to be about forty feet long. He wished he could see her name but it was too dark.

Soon the little Caper was skirting her way through the waves away from the rendezvous point. The sooner they got away the better, thought Dan, but now what? He had seen too much. Now he was an accomplice. If Corker let him go and he told his father it would be like ratting on the person who had saved his life. After all, he had sneaked aboard uninvited.

These thoughts spun around in Dan's head as he sat at the stern on top of the very liquor his father was searching for. Cold blasts of salty night air numbed his face and hands. As if knowing he was cold, the dog jumped up beside him and laid her warm paws and head across Dan's lap. Now he had two friends but what was he going to do about them?

There was a sudden cough, splutter, and final choke and the boat lay dead still.

"Come on, *Martha*, don't fade on me now. I know the Feds are lurkin' about." Corker yanked off the engine box cover. He tightened this, banged that, muttered, coaxed and pleaded. Nothing helped.

Dan inched closer. "What happened?"

"So, the lad has a tongue," said Corker.

Tapping the engine with a wrench, he added, "She's as stubborn as the woman she was named for." He stared into Dan's face. "Had yourself in a fine pickle back there lad."

Dan lowered his head and nodded.

"Keeping the police business in the family, are ya?"

Dan raised his head. "I thought I could...."

Corker butted in. "Chasing gangsters is best left to the big boys. It's a nasty job. Those like Tom and Hugh are plain mean, inside and out."

"Thanks," said Dan. "I'll remember that."

"Isn't too difficult, if ya know how. Those two are real cowards under their tough skins. Step up and show 'em who's boss." Corker swung the wrench under Dan's nose. "Always throws 'em."

"Ya?"

"Ya!"

Dan liked Corker. He even forgave him for

taking his pocket money. "Can you fix the engine?"

"Lad, don't you know who you're talking to?" asked Corker. "First Class Engineer Sergeant MacIsaac, that's me. After Vimy, in the big War, I got meself a cushy job repairing engines for the flying machines."

"Wow," said Dan, impressed. "Did you fly any?"

"Na, that daredevil stuff was for the other guys. Take Billy Bishop, what an Ace, seventy-two German planes to his credit. Never got near his plane. He looked after his own baby."

Dan wanted to hear more and his wide smile encouraged Corker to continue.

"Billy was from Owen Sound, Ontario. Why, he could land a plane as lightly as thistledown. He was a bright young fella. I remember the time he and his leader let three enemy machines get right on their tail. At the last split second they swung around and faced a hellish dogfight. Billy followed a German pilot who was pretending to go down in a spin. The weasel planned to level off and escape lower down. But Billy was ready for him. Unfortunately, the fight had carried him into enemy territory and worse yet, his engine had oiled up and gone dead. As he sank lower, enemy machines guns opened fire." Corker stopped to wipe his brow.

Dan silently cried for the story to continue.

"Where was I?" said Corker. "Oh yes, behind enemy lines. Well now that's where me and Charlie first met Billy. He had managed to land his plane. Then, taking a pistol, he jumped a ditch prepared to defend himself. Now can you imagine the look on me and Charlie's faces when Billy Bishop jumped into our dugout? We screamed, then laughed so hard our sides nearly split. Together we hid his plane behind a clump o' trees so the German artillerymen wouldn't find it.

"Next time I saw Billy he was flying over our trench on Easter Sunday. He attacked five enemy machines. It gave me and Charlie the courage to help take Vimy the next day."

Dan listened to the story filled with wonder and longing. How exciting it would have been to fly into a neatly baited trap only to outsmart your opponent, attack like a hawk and fly away like a hero. He wished he had been part of it all.

The dog began to whine. Corker dropped his tools and leaned over the side of the boat.

"Feds. Quick, lad, do as I tell ya. There's no time to waste!" ordered Corker. "Go into the cabin and bring out the salt bags, buoys, rope, and net." Reaching up, Corker shut off the lantern. "We'll have to work quickly. Do as I tell ya."

In the darkness Dan dragged out the supplies as fast as he could. What if his dad was on board the Federal vessel? He had little time to worry before Corker threw out the next order.

"Fill the nets with the rum I've fished out from the cabin and under the seat. I'll tie the salt bags to the buoys."

Dan could hear a boat cutting through the water. The grinding of an engine and the splashing of waves grew louder. The muscles tightened at the back of his neck. Juices churned in the pit of his stomach.

Finally the buoys and salt bags were tied to the nets. Corker clicked open the blade of a pocket knife. He chuckled as he nicked holes in the corners of the salt bags.

"Help me toss everything overboard, lad. The weight of the bags will hold down the rum and the buoys. The salt will wash out and by mornin' the sea will be a wee bit saltier."

"And then," added Dan, "without the weight of the salt to hold it down, the hidden hooch will float up."

"Aye, lad. True genius is so simple."

So, thought Dan, his father's suspicions were correct. There was a way to throw a stash of liquor overboard and locate it later.

The fishnet splashed into the dark ocean just in time. A voice bellowed through a megaphone across the water.

"This is the police. Stay where you are!" A searchlight blinded Dan.

"Hello, boys," greeted Corker. "Welcome aboard. Plenty o' room."

"Late to be about isn't it? asked the officer. "Wait a minute, aren't you Daniel Veinotte?"

"Yes, sir," Dan blinked, as he recognised Mr. Harnish, his father's assistant.

"Not sure your dad would approve of this."

"No, sir."

"What are you doing with a marauder like Corker?"

"Well I...."

Corker cut in. "The lad and I are takin' a late night cruise. A little star gazing helps clear the head o' troubles."

"It is mighty peculiar," said Mr. Harnish. His small, beady eyes stared down his nose at Dan. He stood in military fashion, feet wide apart, hands on his hips.

"I plan to search this vessel," he said. He nodded his head to a second officer who secured their cruiser to the *Martha-Rae*. Both stepped aboard and together they lifted seats, threw around fishing tackle, and shook the buoys. They ripped open a salt bag, shaking it like a rag mop until its crystal white contents covered the deck. The searchlight shone inside the engine box, down into the bilge pump, and under loose floorboards.

"Guess she's clean," said Mr. Harnish, finally.

Dan stared at the mess.

"These waters aren't safe at night," Mr. Harnish added. "Never know who might be lurking about." He put his hand on Dan's shoulder. "You'd best come along with me, Son. No good can come from hanging around the likes of Mr. MacIsaac."

Dan did not like the way his father's assistant spoke about Corker. There was something about the man that gave Dan the feeling he would never want him on his side in a ballgame.

"Best go, lad," said Corker. Reluctantly, Dan climbed into the cruiser.

"But you know," added Corker, "marauders of long ago had a tradition. When they found a rare piece it was passed among friends as a good-luck token." Corker smiled, then tossed Dan a coin. The cruiser sped away leaving Corker stranded. Even before Dan opened his fist he knew it was the coin he had lost in the cemetery.

9
A Cold Day

Journal entry: *Monday, April 17, '31. Mondays stink. Grounded for a week because I got home after midnight Saturday. Mr. Harnish brought me home but he didn't tell Dad I had been with Corker. Maybe I was wrong. Maybe Mr. Harnish is not such a bad guy. I don't want to tell Dad about Corker until I've had time to figure things out. It seems I've poked my nose in where it doesn't belong and now it's stuck. I want to talk to Mom but I'm not sure what to say.*

Marie called from the kitchen, "Daniel, get ready for school."

Good news, his mother was up and about. Today he would talk to his mom about the lost baby. Dan grabbed his clothes and hurried down the stairs to dress by the warmth of the woodstove. He watched his mom as she stirred the porridge. She moved slowly around the kitchen humming a sad tune. Usually she bustled about smiling even when she scolded. Dan could not bear to see his mom so unhappy.

He looked out of the window. Even the weather was depressing. Fog, cold and damp, had wrapped itself over Seaport. A change of wind could blow it away within the hour or the fog could hang around for days.

"Mom?"

"Yes."

"I … I …"

"Yes."

"I can't find my socks," mumbled Dan. That wasn't what he wanted to say.

"You are sitting on them," replied Marie absently.

Normally this kind of thing would have made them both laugh—not today.

Dan decided to give it one more try. "Mom?"

Marie set the brown sugar on the table. "Daniel?"

"Is it OK if …" Words twisted and stuck in

Dan's throat. "... if I stop at Bob's store for the mail?"

"Darn," he thought. "That's not what I meant to say either."

"Yes, Daniel, but come straight home. Remember what your father said."

"Yes, Ma'am." While eating his breakfast Dan decided that some things, no matter how much they weighed on your mind, might as well be left alone. Before leaving for school he kissed his mother goodbye without being reminded.

"Best take a sweater," said Marie. "Looks as if we are in for a late frost."

It felt good having his mom fussing over him. Perhaps she had forgotten his bad moods every time the baby talk had begun. If only she would stop staring at the flowered wallpaper and talk to him. Then maybe he could find the right words to tell her what was troubling him. It was odd that he and Corker understood each other better, and they weren't even related.

On the way to school Dan thought about his

dad. He wanted to confide in him but the way things stood he knew Corker would get into trouble. Keeping a secret from his dad was like having an angry bear clawing at his insides trying to get out. Dan had never thought the day would come when he could not talk to either of his parents. Why did life suddenly seem to be so difficult?

Shrouds of fog hung over the winding village road like a grey phantom. Dan pressed on toward school. He wished the mist would swallow him up. What if he could step out of the fog and into a different time? He pictured himself high up in the clouds waiting for an enemy flying machine. Then he thought about clearing the dust from the batter's box and wiping his sweating hands on his Yankee uniform. Ahead of him the mist parted. Dan prepared to jump into his dream—only to discover the school house waiting for him.

Miss Spindler stood on the school steps ringing the hand bell. No matter how cold or wet it was, she insisted the students file inside according to their grades. Her raised hand meant silence. Dan's father said she'd had the same routine when he was a boy. The littlest ones entered first and seated themselves in the east room where Miss Barkhouse waited. Outside the older kids danced like a line of jigged cod to warm their toes. Dan scrambled to reach the end of the line before, with a nod from the teacher's head, they were allowed to push their way into the west room.

"Burr, it's cold in here," complained Squirrel.

"You may want to keep your coats on," said Miss Spindler. "There seems to be more trouble with the new furnace."

Everyone grinned from ear to ear. Hopefully this meant another holiday. Unfortunately for the students, the teacher intended to finish her lessons today—especially since her class had ended early on Friday afternoon.

There were spelling lists to copy, multiplication tables to memorize, and history events to be put into order. Fingers were cramped and heads ached. Recess could not arrive too soon. It might be colder outside but at least you could run around to warm up.

When Miss Spindler finally rang the bell the girls headed for the outhouse, while the boys made for the dead oak tree by the alder bushes.

Squirrel jumped up and grabbed a low hanging branch. Swinging by one arm and one leg he looked like a jungle sloth. "Miss Spindler sure can belt out the lessons," he said.

"Ya, she probably stood beside Wolfe at the Fall of Québec," laughed Dan.

Bruce reached into his pocket for a rolled cigarette. "History is dumb. Who needs to know about a bunch of people who have been dead for a hundred years." He blew smoke into Squirrel's face. "Good guys beat bad guys and then become heroes. It makes me sick." He flicked the butt casually over his shoulder and then slipped into the bushes.

Dan signaled to Squirrel. Together they headed back to the schoolhouse.

"Gee," said Dan, "Bruce gets meaner by the day."

"Ya," agreed Squirrel. "Sure would like to see him meet his match though." Neither of the boys could imagine who that might be.

Later that morning as Dan sat huddled in his seat he thought he heard a familiar cry.

A few minutes later Miss Spindler left her lesson to answer a knock on the door.

"Mornin', Miss," said a voice, "hear you have a wee bit o' trouble with the heating."

Dan swung around. He knew he had recognized Corker's voice. He grinned from ear to ear. He was dying to ask Corker how he managed to get back to shore on Saturday night.

Miss Spindler glanced at her students hugging themselves for warmth. She seemed to be a little flustered. And no wonder, Dan thought, for Corker was dressed in his best clothes, his hair slicked back, and his face was so clean it was shiny. "Yes, Mr. MacIsaac," replied Miss Spindler at last, "there seems to be a blockage of some kind."

During the next hour the class paid more attention to Corker's tapping and occasional words of encouragement to the vent than to their lessons. When the children rushed home for lunch, Dan made an excuse to linger behind. He re-copied the spelling list as slowly as possible, avoiding the puzzled glance of his teacher as she sat at her desk marking papers. Seconds dragged into minutes. Dan tapped his fingers impatiently until a "humph" from the teacher hushed him. What was taking Engineer Sergeant MacIsaac so long?

A hand on Dan's shoulder made him start. Watching the doorway for Corker, he had not noticed Miss Spindler approaching his desk.

Pulling up a chair she sat facing him.

"Daniel," she said softly, "how is your mother?"

Dan was so taken by surprise that he could not answer.

"It was sad that she lost her baby, and sometimes it is hard to understand why these things happen. But Daniel, it had nothing to do with you."

While she talked Miss Spindler looked directly at Dan. For the first time he noticed the deep brown color of his teacher's eyes. They looked soft and kind. Had those eyes watched him and read his feelings like an open book? But she was just a spinster teacher. How could she have known what he felt? It had never occurred to Dan that his teacher cared about what went on outside the classroom.

As if again reading his thoughts, Miss Spindler continued, "Some things are never meant to be. We may not understand or agree but we must learn to accept what comes our way." Miss Spindler's hand reached up to hold a locket she wore around her neck. Then, looking over Dan's head, she finished her speech in a soft voice. "Life goes on, with or without that extra someone to love."

What happened next broke not only the conversation but also Miss Spindler's locket. A loud bang from Corker's hammer took the teacher so much by surprise that she jumped up and the chain holding the locket fell away from its clasp.

"Oh dear!" The color drained from Miss Spindler's face as if a plug had been pulled.

Dan had never seen his teacher look so

distraught. "Don't worry, I'll take it to Mr. MacIsaac to fix."

"No!" shouted Miss Spindler so forcefully that Dan sat back down in his chair. "I've had this locket for twenty years and it has never been out of my possession. But I'll leave it with you while I go and ask Mr. MacIsaac for a small pair of pliers." Very carefully she set the locket in Dan's hands, then left for the cellar.

Dan felt a little silly holding a lady's locket and was glad the other kids weren't there to see. He ran his thumb over the delicate design of the oval case, then pulled his fingernail down the groove in the side. The locket clicked open! Although he hadn't meant to, he couldn't help but look inside. On the left was a picture of a beautiful young woman with black hair piled up on the top of her head. On the right was the photograph of a handsome young man who wore a devilish smile and a black derby hat. Who were they?

When the answer hit Dan it was as if a curtain had opened to reveal a secret past.

They were Miss Spindler and Corker when they were younger! At one time they must have known each other, and rather well. For some reason he had married someone else. She on the other hand had never married. That speech she had made about things that were never meant to be must have been about herself.

At the sound of footsteps Dan quickly clicked shut the locket.

"Miss," said Corker, "you should have heat in a wee minute."

Miss Spindler stood holding the pliers. "I'll see to it the schoolboard pays for your service."

"No need, me dear," said Corker. "Call it me civic duty."

For a moment their eyes met. Dan doubted his teacher found the room chilly for her cheeks had suddenly reddened.

10
An Old Debt

That's it! Dan was now convinced that if he could get Miss Spindler and Corker back together again his problems would be over. Miss Spindler would never approve of Corker's nightly rumrunning activities, and if Corker was no longer involved Dan wouldn't have to withhold the evidence he had from his father. How this plan was to be carried out needed more thought, but Dan had a whole long week on curfew to put on his thinking cap.

The days crawled by. Each night, before falling asleep, Dan lay in his bed with his hands behind his head, eyes staring at the ceiling. Saturday arrived without the perfect plan. The job of changing Corker into a suitable suitor for Miss Spindler would be no easy task. But if a prickly caterpillar could change into a silken butterfly, Corker's metamorphosis, though unlikely, was not impossible.

That night Dan vowed to stay awake until he had hatched a match-making scheme. After several hours without an inspiration, he finally drifted into a troubled sleep.

The nightmare he had seemed so real. Corker was leaning against the starboard side of the *Martha-Rae* drinking from his liquor bottle, too drunk to help. Tom had gripped Dan by the shoulders. Hugh was holding him by the bootstraps. On the count of three they swung him over the side of the boat. Down, down he sank, deep into the cold Atlantic. The weight of the ocean pinned his arms. He could not breathe.

"Dad! Dad!"

Dan sat bolt upright in bed. His heart was pounding and his damp nightshirt stuck to his body. Although the floor felt cool Dan crossed the room to open the window. Outside a soft wind swayed the branches of the birch tree. A week on curfew had been tough, but tomorrow was Sunday and a ball game with the gang would put things right. What he needed to do was to think up a good story so his mom would excuse him from church. Dan shook his head—lately life had become one plan after another.

Then he heard the tune carried on the clear night air. Dan had a hunch—if the Widow Wentzell had made a Saturday night date with the deceased, he just had to be there.

It took only seconds to put on his trousers and pull a sweater over his nightshirt. In his pocket he felt the coin Corker had returned to him. Dan took it out and, after a rub for good luck, popped it back deep into his pocket. Heading for the window, Dan was about to make his escape when he remembered something. On impulse he grabbed his journal and scrawled an entry. *April 22, '31: Going to catch me a ghost. After tonight I'll know the Seaport Secret.*

Dan squeezed through the window. He crawled across the veranda roof, shinnied down the birch tree and landed on solid ground. Thank goodness he had left his galoshes on the back porch to dry. The damp boots brought a shiver and a moment of reconsideration. If he was caught out late again it would mean a month without baseball. Should he forget what really wasn't any of his business? No, tonight the missing piece of the puzzle would fall in place. He had to be there!

The mysterious music lured Dan through the wet hayfield like a mermaid calling an unwary sailor. A yellow moon, peeking from behind darkened clouds, guided his way to the dilapidated house on the hill. Never before had the place looked so forbidding.

Silently Dan crept to the parlor window. He could see the Widow's back as she sat on the piano bench singing, her fingers striking the keys, shoulders heaving.

We were sailing along
On Moonlight Bay.
We could hear the voices ringing

They seemed to say,
'You have stolen my heart
Now don't go away.'
As we sang love's old sweet song,
On Moonlight Bay."

The playing was terrible and the singing was worse. It was enough to frighten away any soul, living or dead.

After several choruses, the Widow stopped playing. Softly she called out.

"Dearest, are you here tonight?"

The silence was deafening.

Dan's heart pounded against his ribs. Had he been wrong? Then a slow and hollow voice began to speak.

"I am here, Lyla, me dear."

"Oh!" The Widow swooned, nearly toppling off the piano bench. Mesmerized she appeared to float about the parlor. She looked like a fortune-teller in her brightly colored kimono with her red hair partly tied back by a bandana. As she approached the window Dan ducked out of sight.

"It's good to hear your voice," she said. "If

only I could see you...." When Dan dared to look again she was scouring the place, looking for something or someone. She lifted a candy bowl, looked under the chairs, even under the tasseled shade of the pole lamp.

"Charlie," she continued the conversation with her invisible guest, "hiding money before leaving for the war was very clever. And coming back regular to tell me where it is is mighty kind. Now it's not that I'm ungrateful but where in heavens did you get so much money? Did you nip it from your earnings after fishing trips in the Caper?"

"You could say that," answered the ghostly voice.

"Speaking of your boat," said the Widow, "before you came back to tell me about the money, I was desperately short of cash so I sold the Caper to Robert MacIsaac, he being your best friend and all."

"'Twas a wise thing ya did."

"He renamed it after his own departed wife. Hope ya don't mind?"

"Not at all, 'tis a smart name."

"And since I'm confessing, there's something else you should know. If the spirits talk to each other you likely already know." The Widow sat down and looked into a corner wall. "When you died I was still young and a mite lonely. I married Willie Wentzell." Cringing, the Widow waited for some sign of disapproval. For a time all was quiet—then the voice spoke.

"Ain't natural to be alone. Glad you found someone to share your secrets with, if only for a short time. Shame that Willie died in that August gale before his prime. I heard o' your plight and came back to help. But tonight was me last run with the spirits so to speak. There's enough to keep you going for a long while."

"I thank you," said the Widow, choking back a tear. "If you see Willie give him my love. Dear Charlie, I will miss you."

"And I you, me dear. Now go out to the barn. Lift the third board to the left o' Bess's stall."

"Charlie?"

"Yes."

"Until we meet again." The Widow blew a

kiss into the air. She lit a candle and left the room.

Dan moved away from the window. After that strange performance he was convinced the Widow was not connected to a smuggling ring, but Dan had a funny feeling about this particular ghost.

Outside seemed coal-black after staring into the lighted room. Dan's hands groped along the side of the house and around the corner. He watched the jerky movements of a candle heading toward the barn. His eyes were glued to the light and he did not notice an arm reaching for him from behind. A cold finger cut short his scream.

"Hush, lad, or you'll ruin everything." Corker released his grip only after Dan nodded in agreement.

The groan of a raised floorboard from inside the barn took their attention. Soon the Widow and her bobbing candle returned to the house.

"Come, lad," ordered Corker. "Should have known you'd show up sooner or later." It wasn't until the two were safely over the rise of the hill and half way down the road that Corker began to laugh. It was infectious and Dan found himself joining in.

"Ha, ha, oh my, a wee bit o' excitement almost makes ya feel young again. Shame 'tis over."

"How did you get your voice to drift into the room?" asked Dan.

"Used the drainpipe from the roof," chuckled Corker.

Something occurred to Dan. "The Widow told me only she and Charlie knew their song."

Corker stopped walking. He wiped his forehead, then blew his nose on the well used handkerchief. He was suddenly serious.

"Me and Charlie were stationed together overseas. He was always humming this tune. It kind o' stuck in me head. One night I heard the Widow playin' and decided to take the bottle and get a little closer. I settled near the water barrel and forgettin', began to whistle *their* song. Blimy, if she didn't think I was Charlie's ghost!"

By this time the two marauders had reached

the Anglican cemetery. Talk about his dead friend had darkened Corker's mood. He continued his story after settling himself against his wife's gravestone.

"Charlie died at me side at Vimy Ridge. His last words were of his wife. I promised I'd take care of her. Darn blasted hard thing to do! The Widow is a proud woman." Corker wet his throat with a little rum. "Anyway, when she remarried I was off the hook. I went away for a while till I heard her second husband had drowned. I can scrape a livin' by sellin' me trinkets, but the only way I could keep me promise to Charlie was by playin' the ghost and runnin' a little rum. Now 'tis done."

"What will you do next?" asked Dan.

Corker looked up and seemed surprised to see Dan. The rum was having its effect. "Lad, ya are a noisy night hawk. Don't rightly know and don't rightly care. And anyhow 'tis none o' your business. I'd say we're just about even with secrets." Raising his arm he dismissed Dan. "Go on home. Go!"

Dan knew how Becky must feel when she

was shooed off the field—empty.

Bruce Bealer had been wrong. Good guys don't always become heroes. He started for home but stopped short in his tracks. What about the others involved with the smuggling? Probably Tom and Hugh would not be happy doing Corker's share of the work.

Dan turned back to the cemetery only to find Corker lying flat on his back snoring loudly. A shake did not rouse him. Dan reached into his own pocket. He looked at the coin for a moment then slipped it into the sleeping man's overcoat.

"You'll be needing this more than I will." Unknown to Dan he had just given away his last bit of luck, something he would need on the following day.

11
Becky

"Son, are you getting up?" called Mr. Veinotte from the bottom of the stairs. "We'll all be late for church."

Mrs. Veinotte adjusted her hat in the hall mirror. "Best leave, Nick. Dan should stay in bed until the rash clears up. Odd, I didn't notice it yesterday."

Nick gave his wife a sidelong glance, sighed, then shook his head. "Your mother and I will be back at noon," was all he said.

Bang!

The door was Dan's cue. The downy quilt flew up. He had waited, half dressed, under the covers and had nearly roasted. He hopped over to the window while pulling trousers on over red, cotton longjohns. His parents had taken forever to get ready and leave for church. For him a game of ball sure beat sitting on a hard bench listening to a long sermon. He'd better hurry or Bruce would start the game, with or without him.

First he needed a little vaseline to help stop the itching. He had slept with a mohair scarf over his pillow and now his face and neck were covered with red, itchy dots. It was strange that he could be allergic to something so soft and beautiful. The scarf had been a gift from his aunt in Halifax. At a time when his own parents could barely afford to meet the grocery bill each month, it was an extravagant piece of clothing. Since Christmas, Dan had kept it safe in his bottom drawer. He drew out the beige scarf from under his pillow, where it had been hidden from his mother, and replaced it in his drawer.

It had been raining and outside the mud oozed over the tops of Dan's boots. Running the bases, he thought, would be like taking a mud bath. He jogged down the village road past the Anglican church, where his parents sat inside. He would have picked up the pace but something or someone in the cemetery caught his eye. He thought that perhaps Corker was still sleeping next to his wife's marker but, unknown to Dan, the old man had dragged himself home in the chill of the early morning.

Dan hopped over the stone wall. Instantly he recognized two red pigtails. "What are you doing here, Becky?'

"I'm burying one of my kittens." she said sadly, without looking up. In her hand she held a bent kitchen spoon.

"What happened to my kitten?" demanded Dan.

"First of all, she is not *you*r kitten. You were going to drown them, remember? But if you care to know, the others are fine." Becky continued to scrape at a hole in the ground. "Mama said Rosie was too weak to survive." She pointed the spoon toward a cracker box. Inside lay a very small and very still kitten.

"Sure it's dead?" asked Dan.

"Of course, look." Becky slipped her hand around the tiny body. The head flopped backward like a rag doll. Tenderly she placed the animal back in the box.

Dan could think of nothing to say. He felt sad about the kitten but also he felt badly for Becky. She was a good kid, even if she was a girl. He helped her to dig the hole. Together they put the box in the hole and covered it with dirt.

"There," said Becky, getting to her feet. "That's taken care of." She moved away from the small grave and lay down on a grassy spot that was not too wet, folded her hands on her stomach, and stared up at the clouds.

Dan did the same. They lay for some time in silence. Finally Dan spoke.

"Becky."

"Yes, Dan."

"Are you all right?"

"Fine."

"Sorry about your cat."

"It's OK. I don't really understand why Rosie

had to die, but Miss Spindler once told me there are a lot of questions no one can answer, not even adults."

"You went to Miss Spindler with a dead cat!"

"No, Rosie only died this morning. I haven't seen the teacher since school on Friday."

Dan sat up. "So when?"

Becky took her time choosing the right words to reveal her most private thoughts. "Last year I wrote a story about my dad. I missed him so much it hurt. That same day Miss Spindler kept me after school. I thought she was angry with me."

Dan remembered the day he had sat alone with the teacher while Corker had pounded away at the furnace in the cellar. He recalled how the locket had popped open to reveal the pictures of the handsome couple.

Becky continued, "In my story I had written about the lonely feeling you get when someone you love dies—you know, the one that wakes you up at night. It's so heavy that you can't get back to sleep."

"Yes," thought Dan. He had had similar feelings about his mother's lost baby.

"Well, Miss Spindler said she also had thoughts that crept inside her head when she wasn't expecting them. When she was younger someone had left her. She said there are still times when the feeling of emptiness returns. It was the same way I felt about my dad. So we promised each other that whenever we felt the loneliness squeeze our hearts we would think of the other person and know we weren't alone."

Dan knew that the feeling of guilt, as well as loneliness, could invade your entire body. Many nights this past month he had lain awake, because of unanswered questions pounding inside his head. Why did his mother's baby die? Maybe there weren't any answers. But he did know the reason for Miss Spindler's heartache. Perhaps knowing was harder to handle than not knowing, because now, more than ever, he had to get Corker and Miss Spindler back together. Suddenly he realized Becky was still speaking.

"Dan, do you think it's wrong if knowing other people have problems helps you feel better?"

"No," said Dan calmly. "Knowing about other people's troubles takes our mind off our own troubles for a little while."

"That makes sense," said Becky. "Oh, Dan, I'm glad we had this talk. I was afraid you might laugh at me—you know, like the others at the ball field."

"Guess we were mean," said Dan. He looked at Becky. She was lying back, eyes closed, with a smile curling on her lips. Someday, he thought, I'll let her play ball. And he pictured her holding a bat as he served up a slider.

Becky breathed slowly. She felt completely happy. "Someday," she thought, "maybe Dan will let me play baseball." She pictured him smiling as she pitched a sinker ball across homeplate.

Dan leaned on one elbow. Maybe Becky would have an idea about how to get the courtship of their two friends off the ground. This was a private matter, but hadn't she just confided in him? After all he owed her one. Just talking to her had helped him to stop blaming himself for his mother's miscarriage. It was odd that it took the death of a kitten and a red-headed girl to set things right. But it had, and he knew better than to ask why.

"Becky, there's something you might like to...." Dan's words were cut short when the angry voices startled both children. "Quick," ordered Dan. "Get behind this headstone.

"I tell ya, you're going to make another run."

"And I'm telling you, I ain't!"

Lying on the ground, Dan had a worm's eye view of Corker being pushed into the cemetery by Tom and Hugh.

"The boss don't take kindly to quitters," warned Hugh, as he led Corker by one arm.

"Where is that shouting coming from?" asked Becky. She tried to get up but Dan pushed her roughly onto the wet, grassy dip behind the headstone.

"Shh, by the sound of things Corker is in trouble," whispered Dan.

"Trouble. What kind of trouble?" asked Becky.

"Shhhh." The two children huddled close together and listened.

"Look here, boys, I've done me last run and there's nothing you can say or do to make an old man change his mind." Corker stood firm, in defiance of the two rogues.

"We'll see bout that," snarled Tom. "Hey, what's that noise?" All three men glanced suspiciously in the children's direction.

Dan had little time to think. "Becky, stay hidden until the coast is clear, then go find my dad." Hugh's heavy footsteps crunched closer. Dan popped up suddenly from behind the headstone. Hugh froze for a moment. Recognizing Dan, he took a giant step forward. The scene reminded Dan of the game of statues he and Squirrel often played, only this was no game. Dan tried to keep his own step casual as he headed in Corker's direction while a voice in his head screamed, "Run."

"What are you doing here, boy?" asked Corker. "Told ya I didn't need ya no more."

His eyes flashed an angry warning.

"Thought you might need some help today," answered Dan truthfully.

"Isn't this touching, a no account bum and a lazy deckhand," spat Tom. "Best to take them to the rendezvous at Cross Island and let the boss decide what's to be done with them."

"Cross Island," shouted Dan. A fist cuffed the side of his head.

"Shut up, ya lout," ordered Tom. "Do ya want the whole world to hear?"

"No," thought Dan, "just Becky."

"Best take the old man's boat then," suggested Hugh. Corker was goaded over the cliff and into the sea cave where the *Martha-Rae* lay waiting. Dan was second in line. As he climbed over the rocky ledge he knew both he and Corker were in serious trouble. What horrible punishment did the *boss* have in store for them? Dan's only hope for help depended solely on Becky Wentzell.

12
A Price to Pay

Soon the *Martha-Rae* was skipping her way across the grey Atlantic. Tom and Hugh stood at the helm, protected by the glass windows of the wheelhouse. They joked and jostled each other in a carefree mood as if they were on a family outing. Meanwhile, Corker and Dan huddled close together at the stern of the boat in a somber mood. Corker looked as if a battle had been lost long before the fight had begun. Even the big, black dog sensed trouble and whimpered softly while her master absentmindedly scratched behind her ear.

Ocean swells spewed freezing spray across the bow. Dan had never been so cold—his sweater provided little protection from the icy blast of a northwest gale. The miserable ride was worse than any punishment he could have imagined.

Corker only spoke once. In a low tone he whispered, "I ignored the law to deal with the devils who ran the rum. Always knew there would be a price to pay. Sorry, lad, that ya got mixed up in me mess." With eyes wide and teeth clenched, he turned to face Dan. "Remember what I tell ya. If ya get out o' this one alive, keep your bones honest or you'll answer to me spirit!"

For the rest of the long ride Dan did not know if his teeth rattled from the cold or from Corker's awesome advice.

Tom steered across Mahone Bay and finally nosed the *Martha-Rae* into the protected inlet of a densely wooded island.

Hugh threw out the anchor. "Hey, kid, start pumping. We got ourselves a little wait."

Dan worked the handle on the starboard side, flushing stale bilge out of the hull. His arm soon ached with the strain of the continuous up and down motion but he dared not stop until the pump sucked dry.

Tom, meanwhile, raided the cabin. Proudly he plunked two pint bottles of rum and four tins of peaches on top of the engine box. Hugh added a deck of cards and a pack of Black Cat cigarettes. Soon the two men were cursing their way through a not so friendly game of poker. They bet on their cards with peach halves that they plopped into each other's tin with sharp fishknives.

Dan sat on the deck next to the dog. He lost count of the number of hands dealt and the peaches smacking back and forth. Closing his eyes to shut out the scowling faces he said a little prayer, "Please let Becky get my dad to the right island." He knew there were about 365—one for every day of the year. There was no time for guesswork.

Dan opened his eyes. Streaks of orange from the setting sun melted into the icy blue water and the air grew considerably colder. Dan wished he could shrink to the size of a flea and hop into the warmth of the dog's fur.

After each game Tom scanned the horizon for the rendezvous vessel. And each time he looked at the old man and the young boy as if they were uninvited guests. As three cans of peaches were washed down with a generous amount of rum, Tom and Hugh's voices rose.

Dan watched until finally the two grown men sat clutching their tins containing half a peach each, like prospectors guarding their gold nuggets.

"Your stake ain't no good," snarled Tom.

"'Tis so," argued Hugh.

"Ain't."

"Why not?"

"Got a bite out of it."

"Does not."

"Does so."

When Tom jumped up and threatened to cut his partner's throat for cheating, Dan's hope returned. The two might just be drunk enough to kill each other. However, at that moment a two-masted schooner sailed around the point. Her fore and aft sails billowed majestically in the breeze. Dan could imagine the sleek beauty slipping like a phantom through the fog carrying her liquid cargo away to the States.

Tom waited until the schooner anchored, then motored parallel to her port side. Tossing a line to a man on deck, he yelled, "Tell Percy we got trouble."

Dan's mouth felt sandpaper dry. He looked back the way they had come. Not another boat was in sight. If this was a talking picture show his father's cruiser would now be cutting through the waves to rescue them and arrest the villains. But this was not the talking pictures. It was here and now. His dream from last Saturday night had become a living nightmare.

Soon a tall man with a hooked nose and thin, scowling lips appeared on the deck of the schooner called *Far Reaches*. With one hand holding the rigging for balance and the other resting on a raised knee, the man leaned over and glared down at the crew of the *Martha-Rae*. "Here now, Corker, what's this I hear about you going to the Feds?"

"I ain't going nowhere," replied Corker.

"Got that right," snickered Tom.

"Just ain't hauling the rum no more," continued Corker.

"Ah, b-boss," Hugh's words were slurred from the effects of the rum. "Can't have a b-bum wandering around wagging his tongue about our operation."

"True enough," agreed the captain. "And my sources tell me this lad here is a Canadian officer's son. Now that wasn't too smart."

Dan could not deny that. But who else knew about his outing with Corker? Who could have told the captain about his dad? Dan looked from one sinister face to the next. Someone had seen them together, someone who was friendly with the smugglers—who?

"Leave the lad out of this," warned Corker.

"No, it's too risky," said the captain, straightening up and indicating the matter was settled. "Boys, take care of things, then set course to Miquelon."

"Yes, sir," sang Tom and Hugh gleefully.

Before Dan could protest both he and Corker were thrown into *Martha-Rae's* tiny cabin. The dog bared her teeth and Hugh left her sitting on the cabin roof. From inside Dan heard the sound of the bolt slipping in place and the two rogues jumping aboard the schooner.

"It's just too bad," said Dan, his voice higher than usual. "All we can do is wait until my dad finds us."

A crash of glass as a lantern was tossed on board dispelled any thoughts of safety. Dan could visualize wild, hungry flames licking the deck of the *Martha-Rae*. He could not believe it. To think that only moments before, he had been bone-cold and now they sat in a cabin the size of an oven waiting to be roasted alive. Overhead the dog howled a deafening cry for help. "Too late, girl," whispered Dan.

Pressing his face against the tiny porthole, Dan could see the schooner sailing away at a good clip. There must be something he could do. Could he smash the window and call for help? Frantically he felt for something strong enough to do the job. Tripping over a coil of rope he fell on top of Corker. The old man did not move or moan. Dan realized he must have hit his head when he had been shoved inside. In spite of the growing heat Dan's hands felt clammy.

"Corker, don't die—not here, not now." Tears streamed down Dan's face. He wiped the sweat from his friend's face, then pulled off the overcoat and loosened the shirt. The black derby lay on the floor of the cabin.

In the shadows, Dan saw Corker's eyes look beyond him into a time long past.

"Nurse, nurse, I must return to the lines—my battalion needs me. Tell me now, have me mates gone over the top?"

Dan tried to shake his friend from his delirium. "Help me, Corker. I need you," choked Dan. He turned and pressed salt bags against the door to keep out the smoke. Quickly he returned to the old man's side. "Come back, please."

Corker blinked. His eyes focused on Dan's anxious face. "Oh, lad, 'tis you. What happened?"

Half laughing, half crying, Dan replied, "You were talking to a nurse, a pretty one no doubt—something about a ridge."

"Now I remember, lad," sighed Corker, "I haven't been this hot since the time I had trench fever. Lived in a captured German dugout for six weeks. Shell fire day in and day out." Corker covered his ears as if he still heard the bombing. "Our feet itched with rot from the wet mud. Bloody decay everywhere. The smell o' death stays with ya a long time." He began wiping his hands on his pants and shifting his feet nervously.

"Mr. MacIsaac," Dan shouted. "The boat's on fire! We need fresh air." He found a blunt instrument and began pounding at the glass. But instead of salty sea air acrid smoke from the deck fire rushed into the cabin.

"It's the gas, lad," cried Corker. "What, no masks? Pee into your hankies. 'Tis the only thing we have to cut the mustard gas."

Dan knew Corker had once again turned back the clock thirteen years—he was a soldier who had survived, only to relive the nightmares of war.

The smoke squeezed Dan's throat shut. He

pictured the smoke-filled school. He must get to the baseball lot before Bruce Bealer lost his temper. But the hay field had grown tall and thick. It pressed on his body and smothered his face in darkness.

13
Seaport Secrets

The softness of a downy quilt tucked under his chin and the clean smell of sheets were the first things Dan noticed. He snuggled deeper into the warmth of his bed. What had he been dreaming ... school ... baseball ... Becky? Excited whispers drifted into his private thoughts. The words "lucky to be alive," "a lot of explaining," and "fire on deck," brought him to his senses.

Dan opened his eyes to see only dark shadows. Was it still night? He tried sitting up but a heavy weight pressed on his chest.

He sucked in short gasps of air that hurt his throat and lungs. An acrid smell of smoke stuck in his nostrils. Slowly, pictures of the night's adventure flashed in his head—Tom and Hugh playing for peaches—Captain Percy ordering that he and Corker be "taken care of"—squeezing into a dark place—the sound of a lantern crashing on deck—Corker reliving the horrors of war—somewhere a dog barking—smoke—and then nothing.

The voices continued.

"It was close. Good thing the dog's howling carried across the water."

"Thank the good Lord. They might have been burned to death."

"The fire hadn't done too much damage but the cabin was filled with smoke and that can be the killer. Somehow Mr. MacIsaac managed to keep Dan breathing."

"Almost forgot, that poor man is still in the kitchen."

"Good, I have some questions that need answering."

As his parent's footsteps echoed down the stairs, Dan fitted his flashes of memory with the pieces of conversation he had overheard. Becky must have managed to go for help after

Dan and the rumrunners had disappeared over the rocky ledge at the Anglican cemetery. "Good going, Becky!" The last thing Dan remembered was comforting Corker in the tiny cabin of the *Martha-Rae*. But how was Corker? And what would happen to him now that his father was pointing an accusing finger at him?

Quickly Dan wrapped the quilt around his shoulders and let it trail along the floor as he left his room to creep along the hall. Ignoring the pain in his chest he tiptoed down the stairs, then crouched by the kitchen door to listen. In the soft glow of the pantry light he watched three adults move about and speak their lines as if they were actors in a play. Corker sat slumped in a kitchen chair, his eyes staring into a coffee mug held tightly on his lap. Nick Veinotte loomed over the old man, speaking in a professional monotone voice. Dan's mother fussed about the stove, wiped her hands on her apron, sighed, and shook her head every time someone spoke.

"Let me get this straight, Mr. MacIsaac,"

said Nick. "You ran rum with Percy Brown's gang until your conscience got the better of you. But when the organization learned you wanted out they didn't trust you to keep the code of silence."

"Aye, that's pretty much the story," replied Corker.

"It's bad enough to be party to illegal transactions but you dragged a minor, a boy of eleven—our son—into your dirty business as well!" Nick's voice rose threateningly.

"No, that's not the whole story!" cried Dan, as he stumbled into the room tripping in the folds of the quilt.

"Daniel," said Marie, "get back to bed this instant."

"Young man, I'll deal with you in the morning," ordered Nick.

"Please listen." Dan threw himself on the floor by Corker's feet. "Tell them about the Widow. They already know about the music. Mom and Dad will understand."

For the first time since the interrogation began Corker lifted his head. His playing the part of a ghost and leaving money for the Widow had been an unspoken secret between him and the boy. But when he stared into Dan's innocent face Corker could see that there was not a trace of betrayal. "Oh, lad, 'tis hard to ignore ya. For some reason the saints have drawn us together. Guessed it when ya snuck aboard me boat, knew it when we faced the Maker together."

"Some things are meant to be." Dan thought about his teacher's words and felt very grown up.

"Aye, lad." Corker faced Nick and retold the story he had told Dan. "Before me dearest friend, Charlie Mader, died he asked me to help his wife. She was fine until her second husband, Willie, died in that storm and left her alone with three young ones. That's when I figured I had to keep my promise to Charlie. I tried, but the Widow was too proud to take anything. So I smuggled rum and left the profits where she could find them. Quite by accident she thought Charlie's ghost was the benefactor, conjured by singing their favorite song. Her playing and singing near drove me to join Charlie in the hereafter. But me ears bore the punishment and I kept me promise. It would have been over and done with, except the lad here seemed to be around every corner and was quick to learn o' me travels."

"You mean I nosed in your private business," interrupted Dan. "It was wrong but things got exciting and...."

"Son, why didn't you come to me, especially when you fell in over your head?" Nick sat at the kitchen table, no longer playing the role of officer.

"I thought I could handle it. And I wanted to help you and Corker."

"Daniel, it was an unselfish act on Mr. MacIsaac's part to help the Widow Wentzell, but I can not ignore the fact that he earned the money illegally."

"But, Dad, there must be something we can do!"

Marie, who had been listening silently, felt she had to speak.

"Why not a trade off?" The others turned to

listen. "Percy Brown thinks Mr. MacIsaac is dead so it is safe for Corker to give evidence. And, later, when the trial is over and Brown's in jail, he won't be able to hurt anyone. Nick dear, isn't that how the big boys in Ottawa do things?"

"Great thinking, Mom," said Dan. "We could fix up the *Martha-Rae,* give her a new look. Dad?"

Nick rubbed his hand across his chin. "She also needs a new deck and a new cabin door, not to mention a new engine."

"I'll help paint after school," said Dan eagerly.

Everyone sat still, waiting for Nick's decision.

"Well, if we have enough information, facts that will stick in court, my best man, Harnish, could help plan the nab...."

"Mr. Harnish," said Dan. Wait, think, he told himself. Somehow Percy Brown knew of his friendship with Corker. Tom and Hugh could have told him but how did he know his father was a Preventive Service Officer? An image loomed in front of him like a menacing monster—a face with small eyes, pointed nose, and a sarcastic voice. Dan's gut feelings about the man were right after all.

"Dad, Mr. Harnish is working on both sides of the law."

"Wait a minute, Son."

"Yes, it's true. The night of Mom's miscarriage—I stayed out too long. Remember he brought me home? Well I'd been with Corker. Tonight Percy Brown hinted that someone told him I was your son. Don't you see—Mr. Harnish must be that someone. Tom and Hugh didn't know."

For a moment Nick said nothing. Slowly he rose from the table, crossed the room and stood before the window. His voice was low and sad, as if he was speaking to the darkness rather than to the people in the kitchen. "With each raid the smugglers were always one step ahead of me. But I didn't want to believe that one of my own men could be involved." He turned to face Corker. "Mr. MacIsaac, you could be mighty helpful and I would do everything possible to lighten your sentence. What do you say?"

Corker stuck out his chest. "If the boss was willing to roast me butt, the least I can do is help skin his hide. I owe ya me life such as it is."

"There's something in the storage cellar that might be useful," said Marie. "Nick, come give me a hand."

Dan waited while his parents took a light and headed down the cellar steps. Then he moved closer to Corker. He had a plan of his own. "You know Corker, this new image will mean giving up the bottle." Dan could almost see the hair prickling on the old man's neck. "And as a respectable citizen you might take the fancy of some fine lady."

"Lad, your head is still full of smoke. What are ya babbling about?"

Soon Nick and Marie would be returning. Dan had to get to the point. "Why does Miss Spindler wear your picture next to hers in a locket that she never takes off?"

Corker looked Dan squarely in the eye. "I

swear that someday, lad, you'll be a famous detective."

"The day you came into the schoolhouse to fix the furnace Miss Spindler blushed like a schoolgirl," said Dan.

Corker closed his eyes and let his memory turn back time. "Years ago I was sweet on Catherine Spindler and she on me. Then we had a lover's spat." Corker opened his eyes. "And ya know, lad, I don't recall what the darn argument was even about. Anyway she went off to the lady's finishing school about the time I met Martha. Always thought Catherine would settle for someone more suited than meself. But now ya tell me, all these years she's kept her feelings a well guarded secret."

At that moment Nick and Marie returned from the cellar. Marie's arms were piled high with an assortment of men's clothing. "Mr. MacIsaac, these belonged to my father. It would make me most happy if you would take them."

"That'd be mighty kind o' you, Ma'am," said Corker.

"It's late. Tomorrow we'll make our plans," said Nick. "You can sleep in the cot by the woodstove." He frowned at Dan. "As for you...."

"I'm going, I'm going." Dan headed for the stairs dragging the quilt behind. Tomorrow would be soon enough to hear about a punishment. He took the steps two at a time, burst into his room, and dived under his covers.

14
Surprises

On this particular Monday morning Marie had intended that her son should sleep in. How, she wondered, could that boy get himself into one mishap after another, nearly die in a boat fire, and still want to be in the thick of things today? No, her Daniel had seen enough adventure for one lifetime. She hoped the men's voices and the smell of bacon wouldn't reach upstairs to Dan's room.

But Dan had willed himself to wake up at six o'clock, the time his dad got up. As he dressed quickly he thought of ways to persuade his dad to let him be part of the plan to catch the rumrunners. After all, hadn't he gathered the evidence? Hadn't he flushed out the mole in his father's workforce? Dan would love to see the look on Mr. Harnish's face when he was confronted. And it was because of his snooping (he liked to think of it as investigating) that Corker had agreed to give names and rendezvous locations.

Armed with his arguments Dan bounded down the stairs and slid into his seat at the kitchen table. He ignored his mother's disapproving look.

"Morning, Dad. Morning, Corker."

"Top o' the morning to ya, lad," said Corker cheerfully. He dived into his second serving of eggs, sopping up the yolk with toast and washing it all down with a steaming cup of black coffee. Such a feast!

"How are the plans coming?" Dan tried to make his voice sound as casual as possible.

Nick guessed his son's motives. "Toss out any notion of playing Preventive Officer today. I want your head in your lessons and your feet on shore from now until the end of school in June. This is dangerous work, and I'll not have you worrying your mother. Do I make myself clear?"

"Yes, Sir," mumbled Dan. He should have known better than to think he'd be allowed to join in the action. Dan moved the eggs around on his plate. He had two choices—sit and sulk, or accept the situation and give his dad the last piece of information.

"Dad."

"Daniel, you are not going! That's final."

"Yes, Dad, I know, but there's something else that might help tie up the nab."

"If you've been into more mischief, out with it!" ordered Nick.

"You once told me that after a long chase, when you finally caught up with a suspected rumrunner, there was no rum on board. Well, I know where they stash it." Dan looked at Corker. The old man nodded his approval. "They weight the cargo with salt bags and toss it overboard. Later, when the salt dissolves, up it pops, safe and sound."

Nick looked from Dan to Corker. Both were grinning like Cheshire cats. "Well I'll be...."

The rum was under my nose all the time." He let out a laugh that echoed around the kitchen. Even Marie giggled as she poured coffee for herself. She set her hand on her husband's shoulder.

"And just how do you boys plan on setting the trap to catch the rat?"

"The plan calls for tight lips and the element of surprise." Nick looked mischieviously from one anxious face to another. "Guess I can trust everyone in this room."

Dan nodded. A tickle of excitement started at his hair roots and ran down to the tips of his toes.

"If you want to outsmart an opponent first you need to know how they think and what they would do in a given situation," said Nick. "Thanks to you, Son, I know now that it was Mr. Harnish who tipped off the rumrunners whenever we tried to make a raid."

Dan puffed out his chest.

Nick continued, "A cheat is often a coward. I'm betting Mr. Harnish will not want to spend time behind bars."

Corker jumped into the conversation. "Not to worry, Sir, I've tangled with the enemy many a time. Your Mr. Harnish will be purring out rumrunning routes and places of rendezvous sweet as a kitten."

"Easy Mr. MacIsaac," warned Nick. "Your role in this is just to verify the facts and let us know if Harnish tries to slip in any false information."

"But what about Percy Brown?" asked Dan.

"I plan to sink their operation with a turn of the tide, so to speak," answered Nick.

Dan was puzzled. Then slowly as the plan revealed itself, his eyes widened with excitement. "You mean since they had someone spying on us, you're going to get someone to work for Percy Brown. An undercover agent!"

Marie shook her head, "Nick dear, isn't this game of Cat and Mouse a dangerous one?"

"Yes," agreed Nick, "but there is a new man coming from Ottawa and I've a feeling he can handle the job."

Dan carried his breakfast dishes over to the

sink. "I can hardly wait until tonight to see how things turn out."

Nick buttoned up his uniform jacket. "Sorry, Son, operation 'Switch' will take weeks, maybe months. If we can put the *Lady Luck* and her crew out of commission the wait will be well worth it."

"Shouldn't you and Mr. MacIsaac be off catching those nasty smugglers? And Daniel, I believe you have time to chop some kindling before school—a good chore for my midnight marauder."

Nick kissed his wife goodbye. Corker gulped down the last drop of his coffee. He tipped his cap toward Marie, then looked at Dan.

"About me and Catherine," Corker said, "Don't get your hopes up. We're both set in our ways." His eyes twinkled and he reached into his pocket. "But with a wee bit o' luck, you never know how things will turn out." Corker flipped the coin and caught it. Turning, he hurried after Nick.

Dan followed as far as the open door. He should be happy that things had turned out so well, but it was disappointing to be left behind.

Marie wiped her hands on her apron and put an arm around her son. "Why, Daniel Vienotte, I believe you have grown a good two inches this past month."

Dan said nothing. He straightened his shoulders and marched out to the woodpile. If nothing else he'd chop a grownup's share of kindling.

Keeping his spirits high and chin up proved too difficult. Hours later Dan sat at his school desk, feeling really in the doldrums. Finally, Miss Spindler's handbell clanged the three o'clock dismissal and the children of Seaport shouted with joy.

As usual the gang met at the dirt lot. Squirrel threw a few practice pitches to Dan. Bruce, who never practised, stood leaning on a bat, smoking a cigarette.

"Hello, Dan," called Becky from the bank where she liked to watch the games.

"Hello, Dan. Hello, honey," the others teased.

"No girls allowed," growled Bruce, flicking his butt in Becky's direction. He stomped into a square drawn in the dirt.

Dan slowly walked up to Bruce. "She plays," he said calmly, staring directly into Bruce's eyes. It surprised Dan to discover his opponent was no taller than himself.

The remaining players gathered around. Didn't Dan know he'd be belted across the lot? No one breathed.

Bruce took up a threatening stance but Dan did not flinch. Then the strangest thing happened. The longer Dan stared into the bully's eyes the more nervous Bruce became.

Finally Bruce spat on the ground. "You don't expect me to play with a girl and a bunch of sissies?"

"That's up to you," answered Dan.

There was another pause. The two boys were like sticks of dynamite waiting for a spark.

"Ah, I don't need you. This ain't real ball. It's kids' stuff." Bruce stomped off the lot.

Everyone stood still, mouths gaping, eyes wide in disbelief. A loud whoop from Squirrel broke the spell. Each player clapped Dan heartily on the back. Becky ran across the lot.

Standing close to Dan she thanked him silently.

"Play ball!"

The game proved to be one of the best. Even Squirrel got a chance to bat. The big surprise came when they discovered Becky had a good pitching arm. That suited Squirrel because he liked to play in the outfield. Dan preferred to catch. It was a great game!

All too soon it was time for everyone to go home. Dan was glad he and Becky lived in the same direction. He had something for her.

Becky waited until the others were out of hearing before attacking Dan with a barrage of questions. "What happened to you yesterday? Who were those two terrible men? What did they want?"

"Whoa, you're sputtering like a choked exhaust," said Dan. "Since my dad is working on a case, all I can tell you is that Mr. MacIsaac got himself into a mess with some rumrunners and I wanted to help him. But I couldn't have done it without your help." From inside his jacket, Dan pulled out a beige mohair scarf. "I'd like you to have this, Becky. It's not much for saving my life but it sure would look pretty with your red hair." He practically threw the scarf at her. An awful itch screamed to be scratched.

Becky held the beautiful scarf in her hands. "Oh, Dan, it's so soft." She held it against her cheek. Then she suddenly pushed it back into his arms. "I can't take it—it wouldn't be fair. It wasn't me."

Dan stopped scratching. "What do you mean? Didn't you tell my dad that Corker and I were in trouble and headed for Cross Island."

"Not exactly." Becky turned and began walking down Eisnor Road. Dan had no choice but to follow.

"Becky, how did my dad know where to find us if you didn't tell him?"

Becky bit her lip. She glanced nervously over her shoulder. Spying a crabapple tree she pulled Dan off the road and behind the gnarled trunk. "I trust you with all my secrets, Dan, but what I'm about to tell you is a personal family secret. Swear a spit oath?"

His curiosity piqued, Dan immediately spit

in his left palm, smacked his two hands together, then held up his right hand. "I swear I won't tell a soul, honest."

Relieved, Becky sat down, straightened her dress, took a deep breath, and began. "I did as you asked me—stayed out of sight until you and the men were over the ledge. I waited a minute, then ran to see where everyone had gone. All I saw were rocks and water. Dan, where did you go?"

"There's a cave, I'll take you sometime but first finish your story."

Becky cleared her throat. "What with the gale blowing and all the confusion, I couldn't hear where the two men were taking you. Your parents were still in church and so I ran home. I babbled on about the scene at the cemetery so fast it was a wonder my mom understood a word. But then a funny look came over her face and she told me to go to your house and wait until your parents came home from church. Then I was to tell them that you and Mr. MacIsaac were being held on the *Martha-Rae* against your will and were heading for Cross Island."

"That's impossible," said Dan. "She couldn't have known where we were going."

"Now, Dan," Becky sounded like an impatient parent, "let me finish. This is the part I don't want people to get wind of—they might think my mother has completely lost her mind."

"Ya?"

"Ya."

Unblinking, she continued, "Our house is haunted. The ghost of my mother's first husband lives with us."

Dan tried very hard not to smile. He knew Corker did not want the Widow to know who really whispered into the drainpipe, so he put on his best surprised face. "Really," was all he said.

"Yes," said Becky. "At night, when Mama thinks my brothers and I are asleep, she plays the piano and sings to him. Later Mama meets him in the barn."

"Does he show up very often?"

"Actually none of us has ever seen him. And

he only ever speaks to Mama. Last Saturday he visited her twice. Usually it's only one quick visit and...."

"He came twice?" asked Dan. But that couldn't be, he knew, because he and Corker had walked together to the graveyard. Later the rum had put Corker to sleep—Dan had tried to rouse the old man but he was out cold. He couldn't possibly have made a second call on the Widow.

Becky continued, "All the ghost said on his second visit was, '*Martha-Rae*, Cross Island.' Mama didn't know what it meant until I told her what had happened in the graveyard. I ran to your house and told your dad everything, except of course the part about the ghost."

By the time Becky had finished retelling the events of the previous night, Dan had slumped to the ground. He shook his head in disbelief. If Corker hadn't gone back to the Widow's, it could only mean the second visitor was a real ghost. Could it be? No.... Maybe!

Becky got up and shook her dress.

"Remember, not a word! You promised—it's our secret!" She walked around the crabapple tree and jumped the ditch. Leaving Dan to fathom the story for himself, she waved goodbye and headed homeward.

Dan rose to his feet as if in a dream. He wasn't aware of crossing the hay field on the way home, and he didn't hear his mother's question as he entered the back porch, crossed the kitchen and climbed the stairs. Once alone in his room Dan reached for his journal. So many things had happened since he last wrote in it.

April 24, '31: Today I told Bruce Bealer that Becky gets to play ball. Thought my face would be pushed down to my bootstraps. Funny he just up and left.

Another weird thing happened. I discovered that Corker was pretending to be a ghost so he could leave money for the Widow. But Becky said a real spook helped to save Corker and me from the rumrunners. I'm dying to investigate. Wish I hadn't gone and swore a spit oath. Guess this is one Seaport Secret that's safe—for a while anyway.

Glossary

ACE A combat pilot who has shot down a large number of enemy planes. Billy Bishop was a World War I flying ace.

AFT At, near, or toward the stern of the boat. The liquor was stashed under the aft seat.

AUGUST GALE During two consecutive Augusts, in 1926 and 1927, eight fishing schooners and 135 men were lost during violent gales near Sable Island. Many were entire families of men from Lunenburg and surrounding communities.

BILGE Lowest part of a ship's hull where the water collects. Dan pumped the bilge water from the hull of the *Martha-Rae.*

BOOTLEG Sell, transport, or make liquor unlawfully. Corker carried bootleg liquor aboard the *Martha-Rae*.

BOW The forward part of a ship. Dan hid in the cabin at the bow.

BREADLINE A line of people waiting for food given out by relief workers. Corker often stood in a breadline to get a free meal.

BUOYS An anchored float. The buoys marked where the fishnets were hidden under the water.

CAPER Slang for a Cape Islander, an inshore fishing boat. The *Martha-Rae* was a Caper used for fishing and smuggling rum.

CONTRABAND Goods smuggled illegally into a country. Rum was a contraband substance during the 1920s and early 1930s in Canada and the United States. Many fishing vessels were used to transport the contraband liquor in their hulls.

DERBY A bowler hat. Corker wore a black derby.

DOGFIGHT A combat between individual fighter planes. Billy Bishop took part in many dogfights with German pilots during World War I.

DORY A rowboat with a flat bottom and high sides. The men rowed from the schooner to the shore in a small dory.

FATHOM A unit of measure, two metres. Or, to understand something fully. Dan could not fathom why the Widow Wentzell liked to play the piano late at night.

FILLET A slice of meat or fish without bone or fat. To cut the meat or fish into strips. Fish can be bought whole or in fillets.

GALOSHES A rubber boot. Dan wore his galoshes to keep his feet dry.

HOOCH Slang for any alcoholic drink. The hooch was thrown overboard, weighted down with salt bags.

LANDLUBBER A person not used to being on ships. Sailors often tease city folk by calling them landlubbers.

MARAUDER Someone who goes about in search of plunder. Marie often refers to Dan and Corker as two marauders in search of adventure.

MOTHER SHIP A ship or sailing vessel that is the head of a group of vessels. Late at night the schooners and Capers headed out to the mother ship for their supply of illegal liquor.

MUSTARD GAS A poison gas that causes burns, blindness, and death. During World War I mustard gas was used in the trenches in Europe.

PREVENTIVE SERVICE The organization in charge of preventing the smuggling of illegal liquor during Prohibition until the takeover by the Royal Canadian Mounted Police. Nick Veinotte's job as Preventive Service Officer was to patrol the waters from Halifax to Shelburne, looking for rum smugglers.

PROHIBITION The time during the 1920s and early 1930s when the making or selling of liquor was illegal. In Nova Scotia, prohibition ceased in 1931, and the first liquor store was opened.

RUMRUNNER A person who smuggles liquor into a country. The ship, *The Lady Luck,* was suspected of being used by a rum runner.

STARBOARD On the right side of a ship or

aircraft. Icy waves crashed over the starboard side of the little fishing boat.

STERN The rear of a ship or boat. Bottles were stashed in a small storage area at the stern of the *Martha-Rae.*

STOWAWAY A person who hides on a ship or airplane. Dan decided to be a stowaway on the *Martha-Rae* to discover more about the smuggling operation his father was investigating.

TRENCH FEVER An infectious fever that is transmitted by lice, particularly common among soldiers during World War I. Corker suffered from Trench Fever in 1917 while serving overseas in the Great War.

TWELVE-MILE LIMIT The extent of Canada's control over the ocean off its coasts in 1931. Twelve miles is about 20 kilometres. Today Canada has a 200 mile limit, about 320 kilometres.

VIMY RIDGE The site of a battle in France, during World War I, remembered for the great loss in Canadian lives. Corker served at Vimy Ridge where his best friend was killed.